哈福

哈福

哈福

哈福

可以馬上學會的

超強英語句型課

全方位聽說讀寫訓練法
破解句型密碼、突破瓶頸

一次搞定：TOEIC・TOEFL・IELTS・英檢・學測・會考

附 MP3

蘇盈盈・珊朵拉 —— 合著

哈福

一次搞定：TOEIC、TOEFL、IELTS 英檢、學測、會考

　　隨著國際化的快速趨勢，為了跟上潮流，學好英語，是大家眼前最重要的功課。學英語的好處很多：除了可以開拓自己的眼界、結交更多朋友、獲得多元的第一手消息、瀏覽網站更方便等，影響我們最大的，是精通英語在職場上占盡的優勢！想進國際化的大公司，不會英語那就真是 No way 了！

　　學語言，除了希望可以閱讀、欣賞他國文化外，最希望的當然還是能説出流利道地的外文，跟外國人輕鬆溝通！ 為了讓讀者有更親切的學習環境，本公司特別編撰「可以馬上學會」系列，強力增進您的英語能力。書加外師示範錄音雙管齊下，讓您彈指翻閱之間，英語實力馬上提升！

　　這是一本能有效提升句型實力的優良書籍。本書特別編排了多種不同的情境─工作、居家、旅遊、社交。讓您跟著書中人物， 詹姆士、艾波、辛蒂…一起體驗生活樂趣，並快速飆高英語實力！內容新鮮活潑，除了可以當作您的英語強心劑外，更可立即在日常生活中應用。本書編撰打破傳統單調的條列式句型書模式，每個單元都有實用會話、句型練習、字彙，三段式學習，讓您快速吸收，英語句型過目不忘！

隨著英語教材日漸生活化的趨勢，英語句型亦應打破傳統制式的學習法，以更符合時代需要的技巧來學習。想要有效提升自我英語實力，聽、說、讀、寫全方位加強，本書絕對是你不可或缺的好幫手。除了實質上提升溝通能力外，更具備了趣味性及實用性，能激發讀者自動自發的學習心，達到事半功倍的成果。

　　本書由專業英語作家精心撰寫，道地且精彩，讀來趣味橫生。全書 60 單元的流暢會話，帶您進入英語句型的新境界，跟著作者的精心安排，按部就班學習，英語實力迅速精進。

　　本書內容深入淺出，是一般英語學習者增強句型功力的最佳選擇，也是學生精進英語溝通表達能力的好幫手。

　　隨書附贈MP3，實況模擬，專業錄音，搭配學習，效果加倍！

編者 謹識

最大特色：

1. 原汁原味‧美語文章

為呈現原汁原味的美語文章，特聘請英語教材專家撰寫，內容專業、流暢，用字精練，言簡意賅，看完實力馬上突飛猛進！

2. 句型技巧‧一次學會

各種情境的會話句型，勤加熟讀，英語表達完全無障礙。

3. 嚴謹編撰‧專業錄音

由美籍專業播音員，精心錄製的精質 MP3，發音純正標準，腔調自然符合情境，讓您跟著道地流暢的語調，快速學會正確美式發音。

4. 精讀瀏覽‧同步提升

句型有長有短，涵蓋各類情境的精華，跟著作者精心設計的內容， 彈指翻閱間，英語句型技巧即刻掌握。按部就班跟著本書所設計的學程加以學習，您將迅速進入句型新境界，英語表達能力絕對令人眼睛一亮！

本書架構

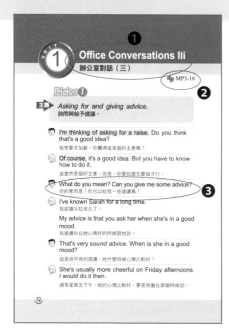

❶ Theme（主題）
每個對話前，都精心歸納出單元學習主題與重點，方便讀者查找，句型使用一目瞭然。

❷ MP3
由美籍專業播音員精心錄製，發音純正標準，腔調自然、符合情境，讓您跟著道地流暢的語調，快速學會正確美式發音。

❸ Dialog（會話）
內容相當生活化，除了可增進讀者閱讀溝通能力外，更可將文中所學的單字、對話運用到生活上，快速提升您的英語表達實力。

❹ 重點句型、單字
套色重點提示，重複練習，實力快速 up，考遍天下無敵手。

❺ Sentences Patterns（句型練習）
精選必考必用句型，重複練習，好記好學，實際運用，英語溝通暢通無阻。

❻ Vocabulary（字彙）
搭配簡潔中譯，重點單字一口氣學會，英語實力更上一層樓。

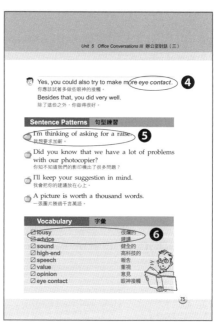

Contents

Contents

Contents

Contents

Contents

Contents

MEMO

1

A New Job
新工作

It's very important to make a good first impression at the interview. Don't forget, the best way to make a good impression is to smile! Preparing and practicing at home will make the interview go more smoothly.

Most people try hard to make "a big *splash*" when they start a new job. But employers say that it's better for new employees to spend the first year just learning about the job. After they know more, they can do more for the company.

在面試時，留下一個良好的第一印象是很重要的。不要忘了，微笑是留下好印象的最好方法。而事先在家裡準備、練習，能使面試進行得更順利。 大多數的人在開始一個新工作的時候，努力的要「一鳴驚人」，但是雇主認為，新人上班第一年最好先熟習工作上的事物。在他們更進入狀況後，才談得上為公司效力。

Telephone Skills
電話應答技巧

MP3-02

Dialog 1

 Making a phone call to a company.
打電話到一間公司。

Good morning, Global Trade. How may I help you?
早安，全球貿易。我能幫您什麼忙嗎？

Good morning. I'm calling about your *newspaper* ad.
早安。我打電話來詢問你們在報紙上登的廣告。

Are you interested in the sales *position*?
您對業務的職位有興趣嗎？

Yes. Has the *position* been filled yet?
對。不曉得這個職缺補上了沒？

No, it hasn't. If you want to apply, please send us your *résumé* and a photo.
還沒有。如果您想應徵，請將履歷及照片寄給我們。

I'll do that right away. Who should I address it to?
我馬上就寄。那我應該把資料寄給誰？

You can address it to our Sales Manager, Sarah Morris.
您可以將資料寄給我們的業務經理，莎拉·莫里斯。

She'll call you for an *interview*.
她會打電話給您，安排面試的時間。

Thank you very much. I appreciate all your help.
非常謝謝你。感謝你的幫忙。

Dialog 2

主題 *Receiving a phone call from a company.*
接到一間公司打來的電話。

May I speak with James Chen, please?
請問詹姆士‧陳在嗎？

Yes, this is James.
我就是。

This is Sarah Morris from Global Trade.
我是全球貿易的莎拉‧莫里斯。

Oh, Ms. Morris. Did you receive my *résumé*?
喔，莫里斯小姐。您有收到我的履歷表嗎？

Yes, and it looks great. I would like to set up an *interview* with you.
有，你的資歷看起來很不錯。我想跟你約個時間面試。

Of course. I'm free anytime this week.
沒問題。我這整個星期都有空。

Then how about Friday morning at 10 am?
那星期五早上十點可以嗎？

 Ten o'clock is perfect. I look forward to meeting you.
十點沒問題。我很期待與您見面。

 *Asking for directions on the telephone.*
在電話中詢問方向。

 Good morning, Global Trade.
早安，全球貿易。

 Hello. Can you tell me how to *reach* your office from the south side?
您好。你能告訴我怎樣由城的南邊到貴公司嗎？

Sure. Just go north on Main Street until Park Drive. That's the fastest way.
當然可以。只要沿著緬因街往北走到公園大道。那是最快的路線。

Oh, I know that area. Which way should I turn?
喔，我對那個地區挺熟的。我應該轉哪個方向？

Turn right. We'll be on the left hand side, beside the park.
右轉。我們在左手邊，公園的旁邊。

Thanks. I won't have any trouble finding it.
謝謝。我應該找得到，沒有問題。

Sentence Patterns　句型練習

I'm calling about your newspaper ad.
我打電話來詢問你們在報紙上登的廣告。

Are you interested in the sales position?
你對業務的職位有興趣嗎？

May I speak with James Chen, please?
請問詹姆士‧陳在嗎？

Ten o'clock is perfect.
十點沒問題。

Vocabulary	字彙
☑ secretary	秘書
☑ newspaper ad	報紙廣告
☑ position	職位
☑ résumé	履歷表
☑ interview	面試
☑ directions	方向
☑ reach	到達

● MP3-03

Dialog 1

 Asking about someone.
詢問個人的近況。

James is reading a newspaper and eating breakfast.
詹姆士一邊看報紙，一邊吃早餐。

Morning, James. What's in the *news* today?
早啊，詹姆士。今天報紙上有什麼新聞？

Nothing *interesting*. Actually, I'm looking for a new job.
沒什麼特別的。事實上，我正在找工作。

Really? When did you quit your last job?
真的？你什麼時候辭掉之前的工作？

About a week ago. It just wasn't *interesting* anymore.

大概一個星期前。之前的工作做起來不再有趣了。

Any luck so far?
（找工作）有什麼進展嗎？

I've actually got an interview at 10 o'clock.
其實我十點有一個面試。

Well then you better get moving. It's already after 9:00!

那你最好動作快一點。現在已經過九點了。

Oh, my Goodness! I lost all track of time.
喔，天啊！我沒有注意到時間。

 Dialog 2

Getting dressed.
著裝準備。

 What do you think of my tie?
你覺得這條領帶怎樣？

Hmmm...it's nice, but it doesn't go with your pants.
嗯……還不錯，可是跟你的褲子不搭。

 I can read between the lines. That means it's ugly, right?
我聽得出你的意思。意思就是很醜，對吧？

No, but why don't you try on the blue one instead?
不是，但是你為什麼不試試那條藍色的？

 Hey, you're right. The blue tie goes much better with this *outfit*.
嘿，你說得對。這條藍色的領帶跟這身衣服搭配起來好多了。

And don't forget to change those socks.
還有，別忘了換襪子。

You can't wear white socks with dress pants.
穿西裝褲不能搭白襪子。

Hey, even I know that. So, how do I look?

嘿，這即使是我也知道。我看起來怎樣？

Ah! Now you look like a million bucks!

啊！你現在看起來像個響噹噹的人物。

Dialog 3

主題

Sharing a secret.

分享秘訣。

Are you nervous?

你緊張嗎？

A little. I always get *butterflies in my stomach* before interviews.

有一點。每次在面試前，我的肚子都會不舒服。

Me too. But I know a way to get rid of those butterflies.

我也是。不過，我知道一個辦法可以讓肚子舒服些。

Really? What's your *secret*?

真的？你的秘訣是什麼？

While I'm waiting to be interviewed, I just *hum* my favorite song.

我會在面試前的等待時間，哼自己最喜歡的歌。

That sounds silly. Does it work?

聽起來很蠢。這有效嗎？

Well, it works for me. It makes me more *relaxed*.
嗯，對我挺有效的。這樣讓我放鬆很多。

I guess it doesn't hurt to try. Wish me luck!
我想試試看也無傷大雅。祝我好運！

Sentence Patterns 句型練習

Any luck so far?
有什麼進展嗎？

I lost all track of time.
我沒有注意到時間。

I can read between the lines.
我聽得出你的意思。

Now you look like a million bucks!
你現在看起來像個響噹噹的人物。

Vocabulary	字彙
☑ impression	印象
☑ news	新聞
☑ interesting	有趣的
☑ outfit	服裝
☑ nervous	緊張的
☑ butterflies in my stomach	肚子不舒服
☑ secret	秘訣
☑ hum	哼唱
☑ relaxed	放鬆的

The Interview
面試

Dialog 1

 主題 *Introducing yourself at a company.*
在公司介紹自己。

Hello, my name is James Chen. I have an interview with Ms. Morris.

你好，我叫詹姆士‧陳。我跟莫里斯小姐有約面試。

Please have a seat, Mr. Chen. Ms. Morris will be with you in a few minutes.

陳先生請坐。莫里斯小姐幾分鐘內就來。

Thank you. I'll use the time to *prepare*.

謝謝你。我可以用這幾分鐘準備一下。

Would you like a cup of coffee?

你要喝咖啡嗎？

I'd love one, if you don't mind.

請給我一杯，如果你不介意的話。

Do you take cream or sugar?

你需要奶精或糖嗎？

I like my coffee black, thank you.

我喜歡黑咖啡，謝謝。

One black coffee coming up!

一杯黑咖啡馬上來。

Dialog 2

主題 *A job interview.*
工作面試。

Good morning, Ms. Morris. I'm delighted to finally meet you.

早安，莫里斯小姐。真高興終於見到你了。

Please, call me Sarah. Ms. Morris is too *formal*.
請叫我莎拉。莫里斯小姐這個稱呼太正式了。

Of course. Thank you for interviewing me, Sarah.
好。謝謝你給我面試的機會，莎拉。

You're welcome. Let's begin, shall we? Do you have any sales *experience*?

不用客氣。那我們就開始了，好嗎？你有任何的銷售經驗嗎？

Yes, I worked at a computer store for over 12 months.

有，我在一家電腦店裡工作了十二個多月。

I was the top salesman for July and August last year.

去年的七月和八月，我是業績最好的售貨員。

That sounds very *impressive*. Can you speak other languages?

這聽起來令人印象深刻。你會說其他的語言嗎？

Yes, I can speak English and Chinese *fluently*.
會，我能説流利的英文和中文。

I can also speak a little bit of French.
我也能説一點法文。

 Great! Your languages will really come in *handy*.
太好了。你的語言能力將會派上用場。

 Dialog 3

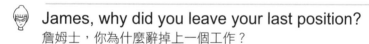
主題 *Further interview questions.*
進一步的面試問題。

James, why did you leave your last position?
詹姆士，你為什麼辭掉上一個工作？

To be honest, it was getting a little boring. I'm looking for a new *challenge*.

老實説，工作開始變得有點無趣。我在尋找新的挑戰。

And what can you bring to this position?
那你對這個工作能貢獻些什麼？

I am a people person. I *get along* well with others.
我是「團體型」的人。我跟其他人處得很好。

Well, that's good to hear. You'll be working closely with many other people.

那是個好消息。你會與很多人密切地合作。

And also, I have excellent computer *skills*.
還有，我相當熟悉電腦的操作使用。

All right, James. That wraps it up. I'll give you a call in the next few days, ok?
好，詹姆士。這樣就可以了。我在接下來的幾天內會打電話給你，好嗎？

Sure. I look forward to hearing from you.
沒問題。期待聽到你的消息。

Sentence Patterns 句型練習

 As they say, practice makes perfect.
就像他們說的，「熟能生巧」。

 Let's begin, shall we?
那我們就開始了，好嗎？

 Well, that's good to hear.
那是個好消息。

That wraps it up.
這樣就可以了。

Vocabulary 字彙

- ☐ **smoothly** 順利地
- ☐ **prepare** 準備
- ☐ **formal** 正式的
- ☐ **experience** 經驗
- ☐ **impressive** 令人印象深刻的
- ☐ **fluently** 流利地
- ☐ **handy** 方便的
- ☐ **challenge** 挑戰
- ☐ **get along** 相處
- ☐ **skill** 技能

● MP3-05

Dialog 1

主題 ▶ *Giving good news.*
捎來好消息。

Good morning, James. This is Sarah calling from Global Trade.
早安，詹姆士。我是全球貿易的莎拉。

Good morning, Ms. Morris. Oh! I mean Sarah.
早安，莫里斯小姐。喔！我是說莎拉。

I have good *news* for you, James.
詹姆士，我有好消息要告訴你。

Really? Do I have the job?
真的嗎？我得到那份工作了嗎？

Almost. We just need to *discuss* the *contract* first.
幾乎是。我們只需要先討論合約的部份。

Well, I'm free anytime.
我隨時都有空。

Then let's meet at the café near our office in 30 minutes.
那我們30分鐘後在公司附近的咖啡廳碰面。

OK. I'm on my way.
好。我馬上就過去。

Discussing a contract.
討論合約。

It's nice to see you again, Sarah.
很高興能再見到你，莎拉。

Likewise. Here's the *contract*.
我也是。這是合約。

Let me have a look.
讓我看一下。

What do you think?
你覺得如何？

It's great, except that *there is no mention* of holidays.

很不錯。只是裡面沒有提到假期。

Really? I must have forgotten to type it in.
真的嗎？我一定是忘了把那一部分打進去。

You will get four weeks holiday every year.
你每年可以休假四個星期。

That sounds good to me. Where do I *sign*?
那聽起來很不錯。我在哪裡簽字？

Right here on the last page. Welcome to the company!

就在最後一頁上。歡迎你成為公司的一員！

Dialog 3

主題 ▶ *Congratulating someone.*
恭喜他人。

Hi, James. You're smiling from ear to ear!
嗨，詹姆士。你笑得很開心喔！

Didn't you hear the *news*? I got the job!
你沒聽到消息嗎？我找到工作了！

Congratulations! How do you feel?
恭喜！你的心情如何？

I'm really happy, but I'm also a bit nervous. It's not going to be an easy job.

我真的很高興，可是也有一點緊張。這個工作不輕鬆。

Don't worry. You'll do fine. Hey, let me buy you dinner.

不要擔心。你沒問題的。嘿，我請你吃晚餐。

Sure. Let's *celebrate*!
好。我們慶祝一下！

What do you want to eat?

你想要吃什麼？

Well, since you're buying, let's go for the most expensive place!

既然是你請客，我們就去最貴的地方吃吧！

Sentence Patterns 句型練習

I have some bad news to tell you.

我有壞消息要告訴你。

I'm on my way.

我馬上就過去。

You're smiling from ear to ear!

你笑得很開心喔！

How do you feel?

你的心情如何？

Vocabulary	字彙
☐ news	新聞
☐ discuss	討論
☐ contract	合約
☐ there is no mention	沒提到
☐ sign	簽字
☐ Congratulations!	恭喜
☐ celebrate	慶祝

The Right Fit
合適的衣服

 Dialog 1

主題 *Choosing a store to shop in.*
選一家店來逛。

Thanks for helping me shop for new work clothes.

謝謝你陪我選購新的上班服裝。

It's my pleasure. Don't you know that shopping is my hobby?

我很樂意。你不知道逛街購物是我的嗜好嗎？

Yes, I've seen your closet. You must have lots of shopping *experience*.

我知道，我看過你的衣櫥。你一定常常逛街購物。

Ha ha ha. A girl needs to dress well, you know.

哈哈哈。你知道的嘛，女孩子需要穿得漂亮。

Of course. Hey, how about this store?

當然。嘿，到這家店看看怎麼樣？

Sure. They're having a *Going Out of Business Sale*.

好啊。他們正在倒店大拍賣。

Excellent. But didn't they have this sale on last month?

太棒了。但是，他們上個月不是就在拍賣了嗎？

Who cares! Everything is 40% off.
誰管他！每樣東西都是六折。

Dialog 2

 主題 *Trying on a shirt.*
試穿襯衫。

 How much is this shirt?
這件襯衫多少錢？

 The regular price is NT$3000, but today it's half price.

定價是三千元，但是今天半價。

 That's still very expensive.
這樣還是很貴。

 Yes, but *you get what you pay for.* It's made of silk and cotton.

沒錯，但是一分錢、一分貨。它是純絲棉製的。

 Do you have anything less expensive?
你們有沒有比較便宜的？

 How about this one? It's made in Hong Kong.
這件怎樣？這是香港製的。

 Ok. Where can I try it on?
那好。我可以在哪裡試穿？

The fitting rooms are near the back of the store. Please call me if you need help.

試衣間在店的後面那邊。如果你需要幫忙，請叫我。

Dialog 3

 Asking for different sizes and colors.
詢問不同的尺寸與顏色。

 How does the shirt fit?
這件襯衫大小剛好嗎？

 It's not the right size. It's very tight around my neck.
它的尺寸不對。脖子的地方非常緊。

 That's only a medium. I'll find a large one for you.
這件是中號。我找一件大號的來給你。

 Does it also come in other colors?
這還有其它的顏色嗎？

 Sure. It comes in blue, white, and beige.
當然。有藍色、白色與卡其色。

 I'll try the beige one, please.
我想試穿卡其色的，謝謝。

James tries on the shirt.
詹姆士試穿襯衫。

That shirt fits you really well.
那件襯衫尺寸剛剛好。

Yes, it's the perfect fit. I'll take it.
是啊，它完全合身。我就買這一件。

Sentence Patterns 句型練習

 Thanks for helping me shop for new work clothes.
謝謝你陪我選購新的上班服裝。

 Everything is 40% off.
每樣東西都是六折

 It's made of silk and cotton.
它是由絲與棉所製成的。

 Does it also come in other colors?
這還有其它的顏色嗎？

Vocabulary 字彙

☐ size	大小；尺寸
☐ going out of business sale	倒店大拍賣
☐ you get what you pay for	一分錢，一分貨
☐ tight	緊的
☐ comes in	有...的貨
☐ beige	卡其色
☐ perfect fit	完全合身

Buying Office Supplies
購買辦公室文具

MP3-07

Dialog ①

 主題 *Making a shopping list.*
列出購物清單。

So I'll need to get a stapler, some *highlighters, Post-It notes, paperclips...*

所以，我需要買一個釘書機、一些螢光筆、隨手貼便條紙、紙夾……

You'll never remember everything. Let's make a shopping list.

你這樣沒辦法記得所有的東西。我們來列一張購物單吧！

Good idea. Uh-oh, do you have a pen and piece of paper?

好主意。呃，你有筆和紙嗎？

Hmmm...you'd better add pens and paper to your list.

嗯……你最好把紙和筆加在你的清單上。

Hey, I know a great *stationery* store downtown.

嘿，我知道在鬧區有一家很棒的文具店。

They've got every possible office supply.

他們什麼辦公室文具都有。

Let's take the subway then. It'll be much faster.

那我們坐地鐵去吧。這樣快多了。

Dialog 2

 主題

Asking for directions around a store.
在商店裡問路。

Can you tell me where I find the business card holders?

你能告訴我，哪裡可以找到名片夾嗎？

They are in *aisle* 22 near the computers.
在第22號走道，靠近電腦區。

This place is so big. Where exactly is that?

這個地方好大。你說的究竟在哪裡？

Just walk down this *aisle* until you get to "Books"
只要沿著這條走道走，一直到「圖書區」就可以了。

And then?
然後呢？

Then turn left, then right and it will be on your *left-hand side.*

然後左轉，再右轉之後，在你左手邊就是了。

Maybe you should give me a map. I'm sure I'll get lost.

或許你應該給我一張地圖。我想我一定會迷路的。

Well, if you get lost you can just look for me for help!

呃，如果迷路的話，你找我就行了！

35

Dialog 3

主題 ▶ *Asking for help.*
要求幫忙。

Excuse me. Could you give me a hand please?
對不起。你能不能幫我一個忙？

Certainly, sir. Are you *interested* in the Palm Pilot?
當然沒問題，先生。你對掌上領航者有興趣？

Yes, how does it work?
對，這怎麼操作？

This *model* is very easy to use.
這款非常容易使用。

You can type in all your information using this pen.
你可以用這枝筆將你所有的資料輸進去。

Wow! That is easy to use. Does it come with a *warranty*?

哇！這真的很容易使用。這有保證書嗎？

It comes with a one-year *warranty*. Would you like to buy it?

這個保證期是一年。你要買嗎？

I'm just looking. Thanks for your time, though.
我只是看看。還是謝謝你的幫忙。

Of course. Just call me if you need anything else.
沒問題。如果你需要其他的東西，叫我就可以了。

Sentence Patterns   句型練習

Can you tell me where I find the business card holders?

你能告訴我，哪裡可以找到名片夾嗎？

Where exactly is that?

到底在哪裡？

Could you give me a hand please?

你能不能幫我一個忙？

I'm just looking.

我只是看看。

Vocabulary   字彙

☑ aisle	走道
☑ stationery	文具
☑ highlighters	螢光筆
☑ Post-It note	隨手貼便條紙
☑ aisle	走道
☑ left-hand side	左手邊
☑ interested	感到興趣的
☑ model	款式
☑ warranty	保證

The New Kid on the Block
新進人員

MP3-08

 主題 *Getting to know the new office.*
熟悉新的辦公室。

 Let me walk you to your new office.
我先帶你去看看你的新辦公室。

 Is it a corner office *overlooking* the park?
是一間位於角落可以俯視整個公園的辦公室嗎？

 Not quite. But it does have a small window *overlooking* the next building.

不完全是。但是，它確實有一個小窗戶可以俯瞰隔壁的建築物。

 Ha ha ha. I can live with that.
哈哈哈，我還可以接受。

 You'll have to share the office with your co-worker, Cindy.

你必須和你的同事，辛蒂，合用這間辦公室。

 No problem. I like to work closely with others.
沒問題。我喜歡與其他人密切的合作。

 Here we are. Welcome to your new office!
我們到了。歡迎到你的新辦公室！

Thank you. I'm anxious to get started.
謝謝你。我非常期待開始工作。

Dialog 2

 主題

Meeting someone new.
認識新的人。

Hi, James. Welcome to Global Trade.
嗨，詹姆士。歡迎到全球貿易來。

It's a pleasure to meet you, Cindy.
很高興認識你，辛蒂。

Let's go for a *tour* of the company.
我們來參觀一下公司。

Sure. This place looks like a *maze.*
好。這地方看起來像一個迷宮。

Well, it's a pretty big office. Over 300 employees work here.

是啊，這是一間挺大的辦公室。有超過三百個員工在這裡工作。

Wow. And everyone looks so busy.
哇！而且，每一個人看起來都很忙。

Don't worry. You'll be just as busy by the end of the week.

別擔心。你到這個週末就會跟他們一樣忙了。

Hmmm...I can't wait.
嗯……我等不及了。

Dialog 3

主題 ▶ *Touring the office.*
參觀辦公室。

And over here is the *photocopy* room.
那邊是影印室。

What's that big office over there?
在那邊的那間大辦公室是什麼？

Oh, that's the boss's office.
喔，那是老闆的辦公室。

Maybe one day that could be MY office!
或許，有一天它會變成我的辦公室！

Good luck! For now. you should be happy with the one *down the hall*.

祝你好運！現在，你應該對走道底的那間辦公室感到開心。

What's *down the hall*?
走道底有什麼？

That's my second office-the *staff lounge*.
那是我的第二辦公室——員工休息室。

Great. I haven't had my morning coffee yet.
太好了。我還沒喝我的晨間咖啡。

Sentence Patterns 句型練習

I can live with that.
我可以忍受。

Here we are.
我們到了。

This place looks like a maze.
這地方看起來像一個迷宮。

Good luck!
祝你好運！

Vocabulary 字彙

☐ a big splash	一鳴驚人
☐ overlooking	俯瞰
☐ tour	巡行;參觀
☐ maze	迷宮
☐ photocopy	影印
☐ down the hall	走道底
☐ staff lounge	員工休息室

Giving Personal Information
給予個人資料

Dialog 1

 主題

Telling someone your birth date.
告訴別人你的生日。

Hi, I'm James Chen. Are you Maggie from the Personnel Department?
嗨，我是詹姆士·陳。你是人事部的瑪姬嗎？

I sure am. I've been expecting you.
我就是。我一直在等你來。

Sarah asked me to answer a few questions for you.
莎拉要我回答你幾個問題。

Yes, it's for our *personal* records. First, where were you born?
是的，我們的人事記錄要用的。首先，你是在哪裡出生？

I am born and raised in Taipei.
我在台北出生長大。

What is your birth date?
你的生日是幾號？

January 15th, 1978.
1978年1月15號。

So that makes you a *Capricorn*. Are you *ambitious*?
那你就是摩羯座囉！你很有企圖心嗎？

Yes, but also *stubborn*.
是啊，但是也很固執。

That's ok. Nobody's perfect.
那沒關係。沒有人是完美的。

Dialog 2

 Asking about and giving health information.
詢問並給予健康方面的資料。

Do you have any health problems?
你有任何健康方面的毛病嗎？

Nothing serious. I have some *allergies*, though.
沒什麼特別嚴重的。不過，我有一些過敏症。

What kind of *allergies*?
哪一種過敏症？

I'm allergic to dust.
我對灰塵過敏。

It sounds like you're very *healthy.*
聽起來你好像非常健康。

Well, I try to exercise every day and I don't have any bad *habits*, except...

嗯，我試著每天運動，而且我沒有壞習慣，除了……

Except what?
除了什麼？

I'm addicted to chocolate!
我愛吃巧克力。

Dialog 3

 Asking about and giving addresses.
詢問並給予地址。

What is your home address?
你家的地址是？

It's 4th Floor, #130 Lakeside Drive.
湖濱大道130號4樓。

And who is your *next of kin*?
你的近親是誰？

My sister, Wendy Chen.
我妹妹，溫蒂‧陳。

Does your family live here?
你的家人住在這裡嗎？

Most of my family lives here, but I have some *relatives* in North America.

我大多數的家人住在這裡，但是，我有一些親戚住在北美。

Maybe you'll get a chance to visit them with this job.
或許藉著這個工作，你會有機會去拜訪他們。

I hope so. I'm keeping my fingers crossed.
希望如此。我祈求有這樣的好運。

Sentence Patterns 句型練習

🍎 I've been expecting you.
我一直在等你來。

🍎 I am born and raised in Taipei.
我在台北出生長大。

🍎 It sounds like you're very healthy.
聽起來你好像非常健康。

🍎 I'm keeping my fingers crossed.
我祈求有這樣的好運。

Vocabulary	字彙
☑ **personal**	個人的
☑ **Personnel Department**	人事部門
☑ **Capricorn**	摩羯座
☑ **ambitious**	有企圖心的
☑ **stubborn**	固執的
☑ **health**	健康
☑ **allergy**	過敏症
☑ **habit**	習慣
☑ **next of kin**	近親
☑ **relative**	親戚

On the Phone
電話中

MP3-10

Dialog 1

 Starting a formal phone conversation.
打一個正式的電話。

Good morning. This is James Chen calling from Global Trade.

早安。我是全球貿易的詹姆士・陳。

May I speak with April Lee please?

請幫我接艾波・李。

This is April speaking. Are you the new salesperson, James?

我就是艾波。你是那個新的業務員嗎，詹姆士？

I sure am. I started yesterday.

我就是。我昨天開始上班。

And you're already working hard. What time is it there?

而且已經開始相當認真的工作了。那邊幾點？

It's 7:00 am here, so it must be 5:00 pm in Vancouver.

這邊是早上七點，那溫哥華那邊一定是下午五點囉！

The *time difference* makes it very hard for us to *communicate*.

時差問題讓我們很難溝通。

Yes it does. It would be better if we could meet in person.

這倒是。如果我們能見面就會比較好。

Will you be coming to Taipei soon?
你近期內會到台北來嗎？

 Yes. I'm coming in about two weeks. We've got lots to talk about.

會，我大概兩個星期內會過去。我們需要討論很多事情。

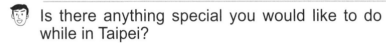
Dialog 2

主題 *Stating wants.*
表達需求。

 Is there anything special you would like to do while in Taipei?

你在台北期間，有什麼特別想做的事情嗎？

 I want to see how your products are made. Can we have a tour of the factory?

我想看看你們產品的製造過程。我們能參觀工廠嗎？

 No problem. You will see that our equipment is very *modern.*

沒問題。你會看到我們的設備相當現代化。

 Also, do you have a company meeting *coming up*?
還有，你們公司最近會舉辦會議嗎？

Yes, we'll have a department meeting at the end of the month. Why?

對啊,我們在月底會有一個部門會議。怎麼了?

I want to get to know your staff.

我想認識你們的同仁。

That's a good idea. You can meet everyone at one time. Anything else?

這是個好主意。你可以一次就認識大家。還有其它的嗎?

I think that's all. It sounds like we'll be very busy.

我想就這樣了。聽起來,我們會很忙。

Dialog 3

 主題

Discussing vacation plans.
討論假期的計畫。

Have you been to Taiwan before?
你以前來過台灣嗎?

No I haven't. But I've heard many wonderful things about Taiwan.

沒有。但是我聽過許多關於台灣很棒的事情。

Why don't you stay an extra few days? I can show you around the island.

你為什麼不多待幾天?我可以帶你參觀這個島。

Thanks for the offer. I would really like to
experience a different country.

謝謝你的提議。我真的想要體驗一個不同的國家。

And I could really use a holiday too!

我也確實需要一個假期。

Hold it. I need to get *approval* from my boss first.

等一下，我得先得到我老闆的同意才行。

Sure. Please let me know when you'll be coming.

那當然。請讓我知道你什麼時候來。

Of course. You'll be hearing from me soon.

當然。你很快就會聽到我的消息的。

Sentence Patterns　句型練習

May I speak with April Lee please?

請幫我接艾波・李。

I sure am.

我就是。

It would be better if we could meet in person.

如果我們能見面就會比較好。

You will see that our equipment is very
modern.

你將會看到我們的設備相當現代化。

Vocabulary	字彙
☑ time difference	時差
☑ communicate	溝通
☑ modern	現代的
☑ coming up	即將發生
☑ experience	體驗
☑ approval	同意

MEMO

Decorating the Office
装潢辦公室

主題 *Choosing a plant for the office.*
為辦公室選一種植物。

 I don't know the first thing about plants.
我對植物一點都不了解。

I must admit I don't have much of a ***green thumb***, either.
我必須承認我對園藝也沒什麼概念。

Hey, what about this one? It's not too big, not too small.
嘿,這一個如何?既不會太大,也不會太小。

It's nice. But I think we should get one that ***hangs*** from the ***ceiling***.
還不錯。但是,我想我們應該找一種可以由天花板垂掛下來的。

Then how about this one? It will look perfect beside the window.
那,這一個呢?放在窗邊正好。

Well done! You have a good eye.
做得好。你真是好眼力。

Dialog 2

 主題

Asking for advice.
尋求建議。

Hi there. Can you tell me how to *take care* of this plant?

嗨！你能告訴我怎樣照顧這棵植物嗎？

Oh, you've picked a good one. Taking care of it is a *snap*.

喔，你選的很好。它很容易照顧的。

So how often should I water it?
那我應該多久澆一次水？

Once a day is enough. But if you forget it can go without water for several days.

一天一次就夠了。不過，如果你忘記了，沒有水它還可以活上好幾天。

That's good. I'm pretty forgetful sometimes. What about sunlight?

那太好了。我有時候很健忘。那陽光呢？

It's best to keep it close to the window. Again, it won't die if you forget.

最好把它靠窗放。但是，如果你忘了，它也不會死。

Well, it seems as if I've chosen the right plant.
嗯，看來我是選對植物了。

One last thing: Don't forget to talk to it. It will be healthier.

最後一件事：別問了跟它說說話。這樣它會比較健康。

Dialog 3

主題
Giving a gift.
送禮物。

Well, I think you have everything you need.
我想你需要的東西都有了。

Oh no. I forgot to get something to hang on the wall.
喔，還沒呢。我忘記買些東西掛在牆上。

Don't worry. I picked out these paintings for you.
別擔心。我為你選了這些畫。

Wow! They're really beautiful. How much were they?
哇！真的很美。多少錢啊？

Don't worry about it. I'd like to buy them for you as a welcome *present*.
別擔心這個了。我買這些給你當作見面禮。

That's so kind of you. Thank you. I think it's going to be great working with you.
你人真好。謝謝你。我想，跟你一起工作一定會很棒。

Sentence Patterns 句型練習

🍎 I don't know the first thing about plants.
我對植物一點都不了解。

🍎 It's not too big, not too small.
它既不會太大，也不會太小。

🍎 You have a good eye.
你真是好眼力。

🍎 It's best to keep it close to the window.
最好把它靠窗放。

Vocabulary	字彙
☑ green thumb	園藝天份
☑ hang	懸掛
☑ ceiling	天花板
☑ take care	照顧
☑ snap	輕鬆的工作
☑ present	禮物

2

Office Situations

辦公室情況

Many companies buy things in bulk and sell them *retail*. A bulk purchase means buying many items for a lower price. Then companies sell them directly to customers for a higher price, which is called *retail*.

Today we have more and more machines to help us, yet we seem to have less and less time. Why is that? Maybe one reason is that we spend so much time trying to fix them!

許多公司大宗購買東西，然後零售出去。大宗購買表示用較低的價格買許多品目，然後這些公司直接將它們以較高的價格賣給顧客，這樣的行為被稱為零售。 現在我們有愈來愈多機器可以幫助我們，但是我們的時間似乎愈來愈少。為什麼呢？其中一個原因或許是我們花太多時間試著去修理它們。

Meeting Someone New

認識別人

MP3-12

Dialog 1

 Starting a conversation.
開始一段對話。

Good morning. My name is James.
早安。我叫詹姆士。

Pleased to meet you, James. I'm Shelley. Are you new here?
很高興認識你，詹姆士。我是雪莉。你是新來的嗎？

I sure am. This is only my second day.
是啊。這是我第二天上班。

Which department do you work in, James?
你在哪一個部門工作，詹姆士？

I'm in the sales and marketing department. What about you?
我在業務行銷部。你呢？

I work with Mr. Liu. I'm his *assistant*.
我跟劉先生一起工作，我是他的助理。

And how is that?
那情況如何？

It's quite busy. Mr. Liu keeps me on my toes.
挺忙的。劉先生讓我完全不得閒。

Dialog 2

 主題 *Asking about work history.*
詢問他人的工作經歷。

So how long have you been with this company?
那你在這間公司工作多久了？

Nearly four years now.
到現在已經快四年了。

That's quite a long time. Where were you before that?

那是一段很長的時間。你之前在哪裡工作？

Before that I was working in a bookstore. It was quite a change to come here.

之前我在一家書店裡工作。到這裡來是一大改變。

I'll say! My last job was also with a computer company. But I found it too slow.

那是當然的！我之前的工作也是在一家電腦公司。但是我覺得它的步調太慢。

Well, you won't find it slow here. You're probably going to be run off your feet!

那，你絕對不會覺得這裡步調緩慢。你大概會把腿給跑斷！

Dialog 3

 主題 *Discussing education.*
討論教育背景。

Did you go to the National University?
你是上國立大學嗎？

I sure did. I *graduated* with a *Science Degree*.
是啊。我拿到理學士學位。

So why didn't you *pursue* a *career* in science?
那你為什麼不在科學界找工作？

Well, I *lost interest* in science after I *graduated*. What did you study?
嗯，因為我在畢業後對科學失去興趣。那你是讀什麼的？

I studied business with a *major* in marketing.
我研究企業，主修行銷。

So you're lucky. You got a job in your field.
那你很幸運。你找到一份屬於你專長領域的工作。

Very lucky indeed. I hope I can do well for this company.
確實是非常幸運。我希望能在這家公司中表現得很好。

Don't worry. I'm sure you will.
別擔心。我相信你會的。

Sentence Patterns 句型練習

🍎 And how is that?
那情況如何？

🍎 I'll say!
那是當然！

🍎 But I found it too slow.
但是我覺得它的步調太慢。

🍎 You're probably going to be run off your feet!
你大概會把腿給跑斷。

Vocabulary	字彙
☑ strike up	開始〈交談〉
☑ obvious	明顯的
☑ assistant	助理
☑ graduated	畢業的
☑ Science Degree	理學士學位
☑ pursue	追求
☑ career	事業
☑ lost interest	失去興趣
☑ major	主修

主題 *Complaining about a computer.*
抱怨電腦的問題。

This stupid computer! It's a piece of junk!
這部笨電腦！這是垃圾！

Take it easy, James. What's wrong with it?
放輕鬆點，詹姆士。它有什麼問題嗎？

Well, every time I open this *program*, the computer shuts down.
呃，每次我執行這個程式，電腦就當機。

What do I do?
我該怎麼辦？

Uh-oh. That happened on my computer once. I had a virus.
噢喔。我的電腦也發生過這樣的情況，那時我電腦中毒。

Well that's not good news. I guess I shouldn't be *downloading* so many songs.
真不妙。或許，我不應該下載那麼多歌曲。

Aha! Serves you right, then!
啊哈，那你是自食惡果了！

Dialog 2

 主題 *Explaining a computer problem.*
解釋電腦的問題。

There! I've gotten rid of the **virus**. It should work like new now.

好啦！我已經解決了病毒的問題。運作起來應該跟新的一樣了。

Thanks, Grace. But I still have one more problem.

謝了，葛莉思。但是，我還有一個問題。

What is it?

什麼問題？

The printer. I get a **paper jam** every time I print something.

是印表機。每次我列印東西都會卡紙。

Let me have a look... Well, I don't see anything wrong with it.

讓我看看……嗯，我看不出有什麼問題。

But there must be. Or else this is just a very cheap model.

但是，一定有的。不然就是因為這台印表機品質不好。

Just make sure the paper isn't stuck together.

你只要先確認紙張沒有黏在一起。

That's a good suggestion.
真是個好建議。

And if the problem continues, just *buzz* me.
如果這個問題持續下去，再通知我。

Thanks Grace. You're a lifesaver.
謝了，葛莉思。你真是我的救命恩人。

Dialog 3

主題 *Discussing how to solve a problem.*
討論如何解決問題。

What? Is the photocopier *down* again?
什麼？影印機又壞了嗎？

Yes. It's always *out of order*.
對。它總是故障。

Maybe we should call the repairman.
或許我們應該請維修人員。

He was just here yesterday.
他昨天才剛來過。

In fact, he comes by at least once a week.
事實上，他一個星期至少來一次。

Then maybe it's time we bought a new copier.
那或許是我們該買一台新影印機的時候了。

Maybe you can make a suggestion to Mr. Liu.
或許你可以向劉先生建議一下。

I've tried. But the company is trying to *cut costs*.
我試過了。但是，公司正在縮減支出。

Sentence Patterns 句型練習

Take it easy, James.
放輕鬆點，詹姆士。

Serves you right, then!
那你是自食惡果了！

Let me have a look...
讓我看看……

You're a lifesaver.
你是我的救命恩人。

Vocabulary 字彙

☑ **more and more** 愈來愈多
☑ **program** 程式
☑ **virus** 病毒
☑ **downloading** 下載
☑ **paper jam** 卡紙
☑ **buzz** 打電話通知
☑ **down** 壞了的
☑ **out of order** 故障的
☑ **cut costs** 縮減支出

MP3-14

Dialog *1*

> 主題 *Asking for permission.*
> 徵求他人同意。

Would you mind if I turned on the air-conditioning?
你介意我開冷氣嗎？

Actually, I'd prefer it if you opened the window instead.
事實上，我希望你能開窗戶就好了。

Sure. Are you feeling ok?
那好。你還好吧？

I think I'm coming down with a cold.
我想我可能快感冒了。

In that case I'll leave the window closed. I'll just go outside for some fresh air.
這樣的話，窗戶還是關著好了。我到外頭吸一些新鮮空氣就可以了。

Honestly, I don't mind that you open the window.
老實說，我不介意你把窗戶打開。

I could use a little fresh air myself.
我也需要一些新鮮的空氣。

Dialog 2

 主題 *Borrowing something.*
借東西。

Hey, Cindy. Could I *borrow* your stapler, please?
嘿，辛蒂。我可以借你的釘書機嗎？

Of course I can *lend* it to you.
當然可以借你啦。

But first you have to return the *calculator* I *lent* to you last week.
但是，你要先把上星期借的計算機還給我。

I'm so sorry. I forgot all about it. Here you go.
對不起。我完全忘了這回事。拿去吧！

And here's your stapler.
這是你要的釘書機。

Thanks a lot. I'll give it back to you as soon as I'm done.
非常謝謝你。我一用完就會馬上還給你。

Don't worry. Take your time.
沒關係。你慢慢來。

Dialog 3

 Asking for a favor.
請人幫忙。

Could you do me a little *favor*?
你可以幫我一點忙嗎？

Sure. What's up?
當然。有什麼事嗎？

I'm thinking of *taking tomorrow off*.
我明天想請假。

Could you telephone a customer for me?
你可以幫我打個電話給一個客戶嗎？

No problem. Just give me the name and number.
沒問題。只要把名字和電話號碼給我就可以了。

Everything is here on this piece of paper.
資料都在這張紙上。

It's really important so don't forget!
這真的很重要，所以別忘了。

I won't forget. But just to be on the safe side, put it on top of your desk.
我不會忘記的。但是，為了安全起見，把那張紙放在你的桌上。

Thanks James. I owe you one.
謝了，詹姆士。我欠你一次。

Anytime, Cindy.
隨時歡迎，辛蒂。

Sentence Patterns　句型練習

🍎 I think I'm coming down with a cold.
我想我可能快感冒了。

🍎 I could use a little fresh air myself.
我也需要一些新鮮的空氣。

🍎 But just to be on the safe side, put it on top of your desk.
但是，為了安全起見，把那張紙放在你的桌上。

🍎 I owe you one.
我欠你一次。

Vocabulary　字彙

☑ polite	有禮貌的
☑ permission	同意
☑ borrow	借（入）
☑ lend	借（出）
☑ calculator	計算機
☑ favor	恩惠
☑ taking tomorrow off	明天請假

Office Conversations II
辦公室對話（二）

MP3-15

Dialog 1

主題 ▶ *Giving an order.*
下命令。

Shelley, can you run an errand for me?
雪莉，你能幫我辦點事嗎？

Is it *urgent*?
是緊急的事嗎？

Yes, I need you to go down to the post office ASAP.
是的，我需要你盡快到郵局一趟。

Do you need to send something quickly?
你有什麼東西急著寄出去嗎？

Courier companies would be faster.
快遞公司會更快一點。

No, I'm expecting to receive a parcel.
不是，我在等一個包裹。

No problem. I'm leaving right now.
沒問題。我現在就去。

Dialog 2

 主題

Giving an apology.
向人道歉。

 Cindy? I have an apology to make.
辛蒂？我要向你道歉。

 What is it?
怎麼了？

 I forgot to call your customer yesterday. I'm really sorry.

我昨天忘了幫你打電話給客戶。我真的很抱歉。

 What!? How could you? I told you how important it was!

什麼！？你怎麼可以？我跟你說過這很重要！

 I know! But it just slipped my mind.
我知道！但是，我就這樣忘了。

I'm truly sorry. I hope you can *forgive* me.
我真的很抱歉。我希望你能原諒我。

 I'd like to, but right now I'm too mad! Talk to me later!

我很想原諒你，可是現在我很生氣！晚點再說吧！

Dialog 3

 主題 ► *Asking for help.*
請人幫忙。

Could you please give me a hand?
能請你幫我一個忙嗎？

Sure. What can I help you with?
當然。我能幫你什麼忙？

Can you help me move the desk closer to the window?

你能幫我把這張桌子移到窗邊嗎？

I'll give it my best shot. You take that end and I'll take this end.

我會盡力的。你抬那一邊，我負責這邊。

Ready...1-2-3 *Lift* !
好，1-2-3抬高。

There. That looks better.
好了。看起來好多了。

Thanks for the helping hand.
謝謝你的幫忙。

No problem. I'm always happy to help a friend in need.

沒問題。我非常樂意幫忙需要幫助的朋友。

Sentence Patterns 句型練習

🍎 Yes, I need you to go down to the post office ASAP.

我需要你盡快到郵局一趟。

🍎 But it just slipped my mind.

但是，我就這樣忘了。

🍎 Could you please give me a hand?

能請你幫我一個忙嗎？

🍎 I'll give it my best shot.

我會盡力的。

Vocabulary 字彙

☑ task	任務
☑ order	命令
☑ urgent	緊急的
☑ courier	快遞
☑ apology	道歉
☑ forgive	原諒
☑ lift	抬

Office Conversations III
辦公室對話（三）

🔘 MP3-16

主題 *Asking for and giving advice.*
詢問與給予建議。

I'm thinking of asking for a raise. Do you think that's a good idea?

我想要求加薪。你覺得這是個好主意嗎？

Of course, it's a good idea. But you have to know how to do it.

這當然是個好主意。但是，你要知道怎麼做才行。

What do you mean? Can you give me some advice?

你的意思是？你可以給我一些建議嗎？

I've known Sarah for a long time.

我認識莎拉很久了。

My advice is that you ask her when she's in a good mood.

我建議你在她心情好的時候跟她說。

That's very *sound* advice. When is she in a good mood?

這是很中肯的建議。她什麼時候心情比較好？

She's usually more cheerful on Friday afternoons. I would do it then.

通常星期五下午，她的心情比較好。要是我會在那個時候說。

Dialog 2

 主題 *Making a suggestion.*
提出建議。

Did you know that we have a lot of problems with our photocopier?
你知不知道我們的影印機出了很多問題？

No, I didn't know that. What's wrong with it?
我並不知道這件事。它有什麼不對勁的地方嗎？

Well, if it's not one thing it's another.
嗯，不是這裡壞，就是那裡壞。

The repairman is always here working on it.
維修人員總是在修理它。

I see. I guess that must make your job difficult.
我知道了。我想，這一定讓你工作起來更不順手。

What do you suggest?
那你有什麼樣的建議呢？

I suggest we buy a *high-end* photocopier.
我建議我們買一台高科技的影印機。

That way we won't have to spend so much time fixing it.
這樣我們就不用花很多時間來修理它。

I'll keep your suggestion in mind.
我會把你的建議放在心上。

But remember, the company is trying to cut costs.
但是記得，公司正在縮減支出。

 Dialog 3

主題 *Offering criticism.*
給予批評。

I'm so glad that meeting is over. What did you think of my *speech*?
我真高興會議結束了。你覺得我的發言如何？

I thought it was great. However, there are a few places you could work on.
我覺得它很棒。但是，有一些地方你可以再改進。

Please let me know what they are. I really *value* your *opinion*.
請告訴我是哪些地方。 我很重視你的意見。

OK. I think you should use more pictures and photos.
好。我想你應該多用一些圖畫和照片。

Right. A picture is worth a thousand words. Anything else?
好。一張圖片勝過千言萬語。還有嗎？

Yes, you could also try to make more *eye contact*.
你應該試著多做些眼神的接觸。

Besides that, you did very well.
除了這些之外，你做得很好。

Sentence Patterns 句型練習

I'm thinking of asking for a raise.
我想要求加薪。

Did you know that we have a lot of problems with our photocopier?
你知不知道我們的影印機出了很多問題？

I'll keep your suggestion in mind.
我會把你的建議放在心上。

A picture is worth a thousand words.
一張圖片勝過千言萬語。

Vocabulary 字彙

☑ lousy	很爛的
☑ advice	建議
☑ sound	健全的
☑ high-end	高科技的
☑ speech	報告
☑ value	重視
☑ opinion	意見
☑ eye contact	眼神接觸

MP3-17

Dialog 1

 主題

> *Giving and accepting a compliment.*
> 給予與接受讚美。

Good morning Cindy. Wow! Look at you!
早安，辛蒂。哇，看看你！

What? What's the matter?
怎麼了？發生了什麼事？

Nothing's the matter. You look amazing today.
沒發生什麼事。你今天看起來好美。

Oh...thanks, but you're just saying that.
喔……謝謝你，但是你只是禮貌的說說而已。

No, I mean it. That's a beautiful outfit you're wearing.

不是，我真的這樣覺得。你穿的衣服真漂亮。

It really *brings out* the color of your eyes.
整體把你眼睛的顏色襯托出來了。

Well, I'm glad you like it. But you'd better stop.
嗯，我很高興你喜歡。但是，你最好停止稱讚我。

You're making me *blush*.
你讓我臉紅起來了。

Dialog 2

 主題

Agreeing.
同意。

I think the company should open a factory in China.

我認為公司應該在中國設廠。

I totally agree. *Labor costs* are much lower in China.

我完全同意。在中國，勞力成本低很多。

What's more, rent would be much cheaper.

再說，租金也會低很多。

My thoughts exactly. We could save over two million dollars a year.

我也是這樣想。我們一年應該可以節省超過兩百萬元。

Then let's look into it. Cindy, can I put you *in charge*?

那讓我們調查一下。辛蒂，我可以交給你負責嗎？

Of course. I'll do my best.
當然可以。我會盡力的。

Dialog 3

 主題 ▶ *Disagreeing.*
不同意。

We're planning to open a factory in China.
我們計畫在中國設廠。

I don't support that idea. China lacks skilled workers.

我不贊成這個主意。中國缺乏具有技能的工人。

I don't agree. We can train them ourselves.
這我不同意。我們可以自己訓練他們。

But the quality of the products will be much lower.
但是，產品的品質會低很多。

We *risk* losing customers.
我們冒著流失顧客的風險。

We need to take that chance.
我們需要賭賭看。

Just think of the money we'll save.
想想看我們能省多少錢。

I don't think it's a good idea at all. In the *long run*, we'll lose money.

我一點都不認為這是個好主意。長久下來，我們還是會賠錢的。

Sentence Patterns 句型練習

🍎 Look at you!
看看你！

🍎 I totally agree.
我完全同意。

🍎 What's more, rent would be much cheaper.
再説，租金也會低很多。

🍎 I don't support that idea.
我不贊成這個主意。

Vocabulary	字彙
☑ compliment	讚美
☑ culture	文化
☑ brings out	襯托出
☑ blush	臉紅
☑ labor costs	勞力成本
☑ in charge	負責
☑ risk	冒風險
☑ long run	長期

Taking Time Off

請假

Dialog 1

 主題 ▶ *Telling someone that you are sick.*
告訴某人你生病了。

You don't look very well today. Are you ok?
你今天看起來不太舒服。你沒事吧?

I have a terrible *headache*. And my throat is *sore*.
我頭痛得厲害。而且我的喉嚨很痛。

You're most likely coming down with a cold.
你可能感冒了。

Everybody's got one now.
現在每個人都感冒了。

You're probably right. My nose is also getting *stuffy*.
你可能說對了。我也稍微有點鼻塞。

Maybe you should take the rest of the day off.
或許你應該馬上請假。

I can't. I'm too far behind in my work.
我不能。我的工作進度已經嚴重落後。

Dialog 2

主題 *Asking for medicine.*
要求藥物治療。

I'm heading out for lunch.
我要出去吃午餐。

Can I get you something from the *pharmacy*?
你要我到藥房幫你買點什麼嗎？

Some *painkillers* would be nice. I usually take *aspirin*.
一些止痛劑就可以了。我通常吃阿斯匹靈。

Do you also want something for your throat?
你需要吃止喉嚨痛的藥嗎？

Ok. Can you pick me up some throat candy?
好啊。你能幫我買一些喉糖回來嗎？

Sure. What flavor do you want-cherry or lemon?
當然可以。你要什麼口味的？櫻桃？檸檬？

Lemon please. And a package of tissue would be useful.
檸檬的。再一盒面紙就更好了。

Dialog 3

主題 ▶ *Asking for time off.*
要求請假。

(knock knock) Mr. Liu? Do you have a minute?
（叩、叩）劉先生？你有空嗎？

Yes, come on in.
有，請進。

I'm feeling a little under the weather.
我覺得有點不舒服。

Do you think I could take today and tomorrow off?
我今天和明天想請假，方便嗎？

Why of course. Have you seen the doctor yet?
當然方便啦。你看過醫生了沒？

Not yet. I'm going there *straight* from here.
還沒。我待會就要直接去看醫生。

Good. Make sure you get enough sleep.
很好。你一定要有充足的睡眠。

And don't forget to drink lots of water.
而且別忘了要多喝水。

I will, sir. Thank you very much.
我會的，老闆。非常謝謝您。

No problem. Just get healthy again.
沒問題。你早點康復就行了。

Sentence Patterns 句型練習

Maybe you should take the rest of the day off.
或許你應該馬上請假。

Do you have a minute?
你有空嗎？

I'm feeling a little under the weather.
我覺得有點不舒服。

Make sure you get enough sleep.
你一定要有充足的睡眠。

Vocabulary	字彙
☑ take time off	請假
☑ stress	壓力
☑ headache	頭痛
☑ sore	疼痛的
☑ stuffy	塞住的
☑ pharmacy	藥房
☑ painkillers	止痛劑
☑ aspirin	阿斯匹靈

Getting a Ride
搭便車

MP3-19

Dialog 1

 Taking a ride.
搭便車。

Can you give me a lift home after work?
下班後你能讓我搭個便車回家嗎？

Where do you live?
你住哪裡？

I live on the south side of town. Do you know where the computer college is?

我住在城的南邊。你知道電腦學院在哪裡嗎？

I sure do. My brother went to that school.
我當然知道。我哥哥之前在那裡上學。

My apartment is just two *blocks* from the school.
我的公寓就在離學校兩條街的地方。

That's on my way. My house is not too far from there.

那裡剛好順路。我的房子離那裡不遠。

Dialog 2

 主題

A carpool.
共乘制。

Did you know that Rebecca and Frank also live in our area?

你知道蕾貝卡和法蘭克也住在我們那一區嗎？

No, I didn't know that.

不，這我不知道。

I was thinking, maybe we should start a carpool.

我在想，或許我們應該共乘一輛車。

What in the world is a carpool?

究竟什麼是共乘制？

Well, *basically* we each *take turns* driving to work.

嗯，基本上就是我們輪流開車送大家上班。

For example, I drive on Mondays and you drive on Tuesdays...

例如：星期一我開車，星期二你開車⋯⋯

I get it. Then we can pick each other up.

我懂了。然後，順道去接其他人。

Yes, that way we only use one car for four people. It causes less pollution.

對，這樣我們四個人只用一台車。污染會減少。

And let's not forget it would save on gas.

而且，別忘了這樣可以節省油費。

Dialog 3

主題 *Going home.*
回家。

Ok, James, I can't *read your mind*. You'll have to tell me where to go.

拜託，詹姆士，我不會讀心術。你必須告訴我往哪裡走。

All right. At the *T-intersection* take a left. Then a *quick right*.

好。在那個T字型路口左轉。然後再快速右轉。

Left...and now a right. These *narrow* streets are really difficult to drive through.

左轉……然後現在右轉。這些狹窄的街道真的很難開車。

Slow down. My place is this apartment building on the right.

慢慢來。我的地方就在這個右邊的公寓大樓裡。

Here you go. *Home sweet home.*
你到家了。回家真好。

Thanks for the ride Cindy. I'd invite you in but my place is a mess.

辛蒂，謝謝你讓我搭便車。我想邀你進來，可是我家很亂。

No problem. Some other time.
沒關係。下次吧！

See you tomorrow morning!
明天早上見。

Sentence Patterns 句型練習

Can you give me a lift home after work?
下班後你能讓我搭個便車回家嗎？

That's on my way.
那裡剛好順路。

I was thinking, maybe we should start a carpool.
我在想，或許我們應該共乘一輛車。

What in the world is a carpool?
究竟什麼是共乘制？

Vocabulary	字彙
☑ **take turns**	輪流
☑ **protect the environment**	保護環境
☑ **blocks**	街區
☑ **basically**	基本上
☑ **for example**	舉例說明
☑ **read your mind**	讀你的心意
☑ **T-intersection**	T字型路口
☑ **quick right**	快速右轉
☑ **narrow**	狹窄的
☑ **home sweet home**	甜蜜的家

Talking to Customers
與顧客交談

MP3-20

Dialog 1

 Taking someone on a tour of a factory.
帶某人參觀工廠。

Wow! What a large factory!
哇！好大的一家工廠！

We have over 250 **people** working here.
我們有超過兩百五十人在這裡工作。

How much can you produce in one year?
你們一年能生產多少產品？

Last year we **produced** over two million computer parts.
去年我們生產超過兩百萬個電腦零件。

Are you planning to **increase** your production this year?
你們今年有計畫要增加你們的產量嗎？

Only if you make a big purchase!
如果你們增加訂單的話！

Ha ha. We'll see, but **so far so good**.
哈哈，看看吧，但是到目前為止，我們很滿意。

Great. Let's continue the tour.
太好了，讓我們繼續參觀。

Dialog 2

主題

Continuing the tour.
繼續參觀。

And over here is the *assembly line*.
那邊是組裝線。

I see that everyone is working very hard.
看起來每個人都很認真在工作。

And none harder than Robbie.
沒有人工作比羅比更認真了。

He works over 20 hours a day without breaks.
他一天工作超過二十小時，中間沒有休息。

Really? That's impossible.
真的？那是不可能的。

I can introduce you to him if you want.
如果你願意的話，我可以把他介紹你認識。

Unfortunately, he's too busy to shake your hand.
不幸的是，他忙得沒時間跟你握手。

This I have to see.
這我一定要見識一下。

Robbie, meet Linda.
羅比，這是琳達。

No wonder. Robbie is a robot!
難怪了。羅比是個機器人。

Dialog 3

主題 *Demonstrating a product.*
展示一個產品。

Can you *demonstrate* your product?
你能展示一下你們的商品嗎？

Of course. This computer has our *modem*.
當然。這部電腦配有我們的數據機。

The other computer has a competitor's *modem*.
另一部電腦裡有競爭廠商的數據機。

James tests both computers.
詹姆士測試兩部電腦。

I see. Your *modem* is much faster than the competitor's.
我了解了。你們的數據機比競爭廠商的快得多。

Not only is it faster, but it's also cheaper.
它不僅快得多，也比較便宜。

That's exactly what we want to buy.
這就是我們之所以要買的原因。

Perfect. Now there's only one thing left to talk about: the price.

太好了。現在只剩一件事可以討論了：價格。

Sentence Patterns 句型練習

Are you planning to increase your production this year?

你們今年有計畫要增加你們的產量嗎？

This I have to see.

這我一定要見識一下。

Can you demonstrate your product?

你能展示一下你們的商品？

Not only is it faster, but it's also cheaper.

它不僅快得多，也比較便宜。

Vocabulary 字彙

☐ successful	成功的
☐ relationships	關係
☐ produce	生產
☐ increase	增加
☐ so far so good	到目前為止都很好
☐ assembly line	組裝線
☐ no wonder	難怪
☐ demonstrate	展示
☐ modem	數據機

Prices
價格

Dialog *1*

 主題 *Offering a discount.*
打折。

How much are you willing to sell your product for?
你的商品希望賣多少錢？

Our modems sell for $50 retail.
我們數據機的零售價是五十元一個。

What if we buy them in bulk?
如果我們大宗買呢？

We have a bulk *discount* of 40%. So the price is $30 *per unit.*

大宗買我們可以打六折。這樣，一個就是三十塊。

And how many units would we have to purchase?
那，我們需要買多少個？

You will have to purchase a *minimum* of 100,000 units.

你們一次最少需要買十萬個。

But 100,000 is way too many!
但是，十萬個太多了。

Dialog 2

主題 ▶ *Bargaining.*
討價還價。

Even at the bulk price, it is still too high.
即使是大宗的價格都還是太高了。

But you saw for yourself. Our product is very high quality.
但是，你自己看到了。我們的產品品質很好。

But at that price I can't cover my costs.
但是，這樣的價格不敷成本。

Could you please lower the price a little bit more?
你的價格可以再降一點嗎？

How much are you willing to pay?
你願意付多少錢？

I can pay a *maximum* of $27 for each unit.
我一個單位最高可以付二十七元。

Well, I will have to check with my *supervisor*.
那，我需要跟我的主管討論一下。

Please wait a minute while I call her.
我去找她，請等一下。

Dialog 3

 主題 ▶ *Agreeing to a price.*
同意某一個價格。

I just spoke with my *supervisor*. The lowest we can go is $28 *per unit*.

我剛跟我的主管談過了。我們最低能給二十八元。

Are there any other *details* I should know about?

還有哪些細節是我該知道的？

With this special price you will have to give a *down payment.*

因為特價，你需要先付頭期款。

How much is the *down payment*?

頭期款需要多少錢？

You will have to pay 50% today and 50% *on delivery*.

你今天必須先付一半訂金，送貨後再付餘款。

I will have to think about it. Let me get back to you.

我必須先考慮一下。我再給你回覆。

Sentence Patterns 句型練習

How much are you willing to sell your product for?

你的商品希望賣多少錢？

Even at the bulk price, it is still too high.

即使是大宗的價格都還是太高了。

But you saw for yourself.

但是，你自己看到了。

Let me get back to you.

我再給你回覆。

Vocabulary 字彙

☑ directly	直接地
☑ discount	折扣
☑ per unit	每一單位
☑ minimum	最低（價、量）
☑ maximum	最高（價、量）
☑ supervisor	主管
☑ details	細節
☑ down payment	頭期款
☑ on delivery	貨到（付款）

MEMO

3

Going Abroad
出國

Before leaving the country, you must have a passport. A passport allows you to travel abroad and to re-enter the country. A visa, on the other hand, is given by the country that you want to travel to.

Airports usually have different terminals. For example, international flights leave from the international terminal and domestic flights leave from the domestic terminal. There may also be an arrivals terminal and a departures terminal.

在出國之前，你必須有護照。護照是讓你出境旅行，回國入境的通行證。另外，簽證則是由你旅行的目的地國家所發給。 機場通常有不同的航站大廈。例如：國際線的航班由國際線航站大廈離境，而國內的航班則由國內線航站大廈離開。也會有離境和抵達的航站大廈。

Applying for a Passport
申請護照

MP3-22

Dialog 1

 Asking for an application.
索取申請表。

Good afternoon. I would like to apply for a passport.
午安。我要申請護照。

Have you *filled out* an *application form*?
你填申請表了嗎?

Not yet. What do I need to apply?
還沒。申請需要什麼東西?

Besides the *application form*, you will need two passport photos.
除了申請表之外,你需要兩張護照用的照片。

And how much will it cost?
申請費用是多少錢?

It is $100. It will also take between one and two weeks to *process*.
一百元。我們需要一到兩個星期來處理申請。

But I want to leave in two weeks! Will it be ready in time?
但是,我希望二個禮拜後就出發了!到時候護照就好了嗎?

Your guess is as good as mine. Just apply as soon as you can.

你算得跟我一樣準。你只要儘早申請就好了。

Dialog 2

 Getting a photo taken.
拍照。

 Welcome to Jim's One Hour Photo. How can I help you?

歡迎光臨吉姆一小時快照店。我能幫什麼忙嗎？

 I would like two passport photos as soon as possible.
我想要盡快拿到兩張護照用的照片。

 No problem. Please have a seat and look *straight* into the camera.

沒問題。請坐，面向鏡頭。

 Not so fast! How is my hair? I didn't even put on *make up* today!

等一下！我的頭髮看起來怎樣？我今天根本沒化妝！

 Don't worry. You look wonderful. Say cheese!
別擔心。你看起來好極了。笑一個！

 Cheeeeeese. (flash) How long will the photos take?

嘻——（閃光）。照片要花多久時間處理？

They'll be ready in 45 minutes.
四十五分鐘內就好了。

 Great. That gives me time to fill out the *application form.*
太好了。這樣我就有時間填申請表。

I'll see you in 45 minutes.
我四十五分鐘後回來。

Dialog 3

 主題 *Picking up the passport.*
領護照。

10 days later.
十天後。

 Good morning. I'm here to pick up my passport.
早安。我來領我的護照。

 Can I have your full name, please?
請問你的全名？

 My name is April Lee. A-P-R-I-L, L-E-E. I *submitted* my application ten days ago.
我的名字是艾波・李。我十天前提出申請的。

 Then it should be ready. Can I *confirm* your date of birth?
那應該已經好了。我可以跟你確認一下生日嗎？

My birth date is February 10, 1975.

我的生日是1975年2月10日。

Ah- here it is. Where are you going?

啊，找到了。你要去哪裡？

I'm going to Taiwan in two days. That's why I'm in such a hurry.

我兩天後要到台灣去。這就是我那麼急的原因。

I've heard that's a beautiful country. Have a good time!

我聽說那是個很漂亮的地方。祝你玩得開心！

I would like to apply for a passport.

我要申請護照。

Besides the application form, you will need two passport photos.

除了申請表之外，你需要兩張護照用的照片。

Your guess is as good as mine.

你的猜想跟我的差不多。

I'm here to pick up my passport.

我來領我的護照。

Vocabulary	字彙
☑ filled out	填寫
☑ application form	申請表
☑ process	處理
☑ straight	直直地
☑ make up	化妝
☑ submitted	繳交
☑ confirm	確認

MEMO

UNIT 2 At the Travel Agency

在旅行社

MP3-23

 Dialog 1

主題 *Stating travel dates.*
說出旅行的日期。

Hi, there. I would like to book a flight to Taipei, Taiwan.
你好。我要訂到台灣台北的機票。

When would you like to *depart*?
你打算什麼時候出發？

I want to *depart* next Monday. That would be February 3rd.

我想要在下個星期一出發。就是2月3日。

That's a very busy time, you know. You'll arrive just before Chinese New Year.

你知道，現在正是旺季。你正好趕在中國新年前抵達。

Really? That sounds so exciting!
真的？聽起來很刺激！

I *doubt* there are any seats left for that date. Let me check the computer.

恐怕那天沒有位子了。讓我查一下電腦。

This is a very important trip. I really hope I can get a seat.

這是一趟很重要的旅行。我真的希望我能訂到位子。

Oh! This must be your lucky day! There was just a *cancellation*.

喔，今天一定是你的幸運日！剛好有人取消訂位了。

Dialog 2

主題 *Stating preferences for a plane trip.*
告訴他人飛行行程上的偏好。

Your departure date is now *confirmed*. When would you like to return?

你的出發日期已經確定了。你要什麼時候回來？

I would like to return two weeks from the third. That would be the 17th.

我想在從3號算起的兩個星期後回來。就是17號。

And do you prefer a window or an aisle seat?

那你想要靠窗還是靠走道的位子？

Window please. I want to sleep all the way there.

靠窗的。我想一路睡到台灣。

And are you a vegetarian?

你吃素嗎？

I'll have the vegetarian dish please.

請幫我訂素食餐。

OK then. You have a *confirmed* flight with Japan Airlines *departing* Monday and returning on the 17th.

好。你星期一出發，回程為17日的日本航空機位已經確認了。

Excellent. Everything is going so well. It must be my lucky day.

太好了。每件事情都進行得很順利。今天一定是我的幸運日。

Dialog 3

 Discussing a method of payment.
討論付款方式。

Now there's just one more detail. How would you like to pay for this?

現在只有一個細節需要確定。你要怎麼付款？

Let me see. You have your choice of Visa, American Express or Mastercard.

我看看。你可以選Visa卡、美國運通卡或者萬事達卡。

We accept all of them. You can also use your *ATM card.*

我們都收。我們也可以用金融提款卡。

Oh! Before I forget, please print off a *receipt* for my company.

喔，差點忘記了，請給我張收據，可以拿回公司報帳。

Certainly. Here is your *receipt* and an *itinerary*. Have a good trip.

那當然。這是你的收據以及行程表。祝你旅途愉快。

Thank you so much for your help.
非常感謝你的幫忙。

Sentence Patterns 句型練習

That sounds so exciting!
聽起來很刺激！

This must be your lucky day!
今天一定是你的幸運日！

And do you prefer a window or an aisle seat?
那你喜歡靠窗還是靠走道的位子？

You have your choice of Visa, American Express or Mastercard.
你可以選Visa卡、美國運通卡或者萬事達卡。

Vocabulary	字彙
☑ fare	交通費用
☑ depart	出發
☑ arrive	抵達
☑ doubt	懷疑
☑ cancellation	取消
☑ confirmed	確認的
☑ ATM card	金融提款卡
☑ receipt	收據
☑ itinerary	行程表

Packing
打包

MP3-24

Dialog 1

主題 *Talking about suitcases.*
討論旅行箱。

Honey, can I use your big suitcase?
親愛的，我可以用你的大旅行箱嗎？

You mean the *expandable* one?
你是說那個可以擴大的那一個？

Yes, there's a whole pile of clothes I need to fit inside.
對，因為我有一大堆衣服要裝。

But you're just going for a couple of weeks.
但是，你只去兩個星期。

Do you really need such a big suitcase?
真的需要這麼大的箱子嗎？

If you want any souvenirs at all you'd better give me the bag!
如果你想要得到紀念品，你最好還是把袋子給我。

Oh, in that case you can also use my *carry-on* bag.
喔，這樣的話，你也可以用我的手提袋。

Dialog ❷

主題 ▶ *Deciding what to pack.*
決定該打包的東西。

Should I take my jacket?
我應該帶夾克嗎？

But it's the middle of the summer. And Taiwan is a *tropical* island!
但是，現在是夏天。而台灣是個熱帶島嶼。

Yes, but it also has very tall mountains.
對，可是它也有很高的山。

What I if spend a night in the mountains?
要是我在山上過夜的話怎麼辦？

Then you should consider taking it. You still have lots of room.
那你就應該考慮帶著它。你還有很多空位可以裝。

Yes, better safe than sorry.
對，預防萬一，免得後悔。

But the problem is whether or not you can lift it.
但是，問題是你拿不拿得動。

Dialog 3

主題 *Packing for emergencies.*
為緊急狀況打包準備。

There! I'm finally done.
你看！我終於打包完了。

Don't forget to pack your carry-on bag.
別忘了打包你的手提袋。

I've already packed everything inside the big suitcase.
我已經把所有東西放進大行李箱裡了。

What should I put in the carry-on?
手提袋要裝什麼？

I usually put a book, my *toiletries* and *a change of clothes.*
我通常會放一本書，盥洗用品以及替換的衣服。

Why do you put *toiletries* and clothes in your *carry-on* bag?
你為什麼在手提袋裡放盥洗用品以及替換的衣服？

Just in case they lose my luggage. Then at least I'm prepared.
以防他們把我的行李寄丟了，這樣至少我有所準備。

Sentence Patterns　句型練習

Do you really need such a big suitcase?
你真的需要這麼大的一個箱子嗎？

What if I spend a night in the mountains?
要是我在山上過夜的話怎麼辦？

Yes, better safe than sorry.
對，預防萬一，免得後悔。

Just in case they lose my luggage.
以防他們把我的行李寄丟了。

Vocabulary	字彙
☑ rush	趕
☑ last-minute	最後一分鐘的
☑ expandable	可以擴大的
☑ carry-on	手提的
☑ tropical	熱帶的
☑ toiletries	盥洗用品
☑ a change of clothes	替換的衣服

🔘 MP3-25

 Dialog 1

主題 *Checking in.*
辦理登機手續。

Good morning. I'm checking in for Flight JAL 123 to Taipei.
早，我要辦理飛到台北的JAL 123班機的登機手續。

Here's my ticket and passport.
這是我的機票和護照。

How many pieces of luggage will you be checking in?
您有幾件行李需要托運？

Just one. I'm only going for two weeks.
只有一件。我只去兩個星期。

Did you pack the luggage yourself?
您是自己打包行李的嗎？

Yes, of course. Why do you ask?
當然。你為什麼問？

Well, you don't want to be caught with anything *illegal* in your bag.
呃，您不會希望行李裡被查出什麼違禁品吧。

The *penalties* are very serious.
這個罰責是很重的。

Well, there's nothing to worry about. I packed everything myself.

喔，沒什麼好擔心的。每一樣東西都是我自己打包的。

Here are your luggage tags then.
這是您的行李托運標籤。

You're bags have been checked all the way through to Taipei.
您的行李會一路托運到台北。

Dialog 2

 主題

Instructions for transiting.
轉機的指示。

There's been a last minute change. You will have to transit in Tokyo before flying on to Taipei.
有一個臨時的變動。您在飛到台北之前，必須在東京轉機。

Oh, no. I hope the *stopover* is not too long.
喔，不。我希望轉機的等候時間不會太長。

Unfortunately, you will have to spend the night in Tokyo.
不幸的是，您將會在東京停留一個晚上。

Your *connecting flight* is at noon the following day.
您的轉接班機在第二天的中午。

 Wait a minute!
等一下！

There's no way I'm going to spend the night in the airport.
要我在機場待一晚是不可能的。

I bought a direct flight.
我買了直飛的機票。

 Yes, I understand that and I apologize.
這我知道，我很抱歉。

That's why we are providing you with this hotel *voucher*.
所以我們會提供您住宿招待券。

 It better include meals and transportation to and from the airport.
它最好包括餐點以及來往機場的交通費用。

 Yes, it does. I'm very sorry for the inconvenience.
當然包括在內。很抱歉造成您的不便。

 (Sigh.)This is going to be a long flight.
（嘆氣）這將是一段冗長的飛行。

Dialog 3

 主題 ▶ *Going through the security check.*
通過安全檢查。

 Please put all *metal* objects in the box please.
請將所有金屬製品放在這個盒子裡。

We need to x-ray them.
我們需要X光的檢查。

 Of course. Will the x-ray ruin the film in my camera?
當然。Ｘ光會弄壞我照相機裡的底片嗎？

 You have nothing to worry about. Our machines won't harm your film.
你什麼都不用擔心。我們的機器不會弄壞你的底片。

April walks through-BEEEEEEP!
艾波走過去，嗶—嗶—！

 Oh no! Did I do something wrong?
喔，不！我做錯什麼事了嗎？

 Hold out your arms please. Hmm... I see what's causing the problem.
請把手臂張開。嗯……我知道問題出在哪裡了。

 Oh, I'm sorry. I forgot to take the change out of my pocket.
喔，很抱歉。我忘了把口袋裡的零錢拿出來。

114

Sentence Patterns 句型練習

Why do you ask?
你為什麼問？

I hope the stopover is not too long.
我希望轉機的等候時間不會太長。

There's no way I'm going to spend the night in the airport.
要我在機場待一晚是不可能的。

I forgot to take the change out of my pocket.
我忘了把口袋裡的零錢拿出來。

Vocabulary	字彙
☑ boarding pass	登機證
☑ gate	登機門
☑ illegal	違法的
☑ penalties	處罰
☑ luggage tag	行李標籤
☑ stopover	轉機等待
☑ connecting flight	轉接的飛機
☑ voucher	招待券
☑ security	安全
☑ metal	金屬的

On the Plane
在飛機上

MP3-26

Dialog 1

 主題 ▶ *Asking for something from the flight attendant.*
向空服員索取東西。

Could I get an English newspaper please?
能不能請你幫我拿一份英文報紙？

I think we're all out of English papers.
我想我們的英文報紙已經沒有了。

But there are still some magazines left.
但是，還有一些雜誌。

Which ones?
哪些雜誌？

Oh, the usual: Business Week, Time and Newsweek...
喔，商業週刊、時代雜誌和新聞週刊……

Can you check to see if you have this month's National Geographic?
你能不能看看有沒有這個月的國家地理雜誌？

Let me look up in *First Class*. I'm sure there's one up there.
我到頭等艙去看看。我記得那裡有一本。

116

Thank you. I really appreciate it.
謝謝你。非常感謝你的幫忙。

 No problem. I'll be right back.
沒問題。我馬上回來。

 Dialog 2

 Being served a meal on the plane.
在飛機上用餐。

 Excuse me, madam. Could you please put your seat *upright*?

不好意思，小姐。能否請您將座椅直立起來？

 Oh. I must have *nodded off*. Is it dinner time already?

喔，我一定是睡著了。已經是晚餐時間了嗎？

 Yes, would you like chicken or fish?
是的，您要雞肉還是魚？

 I thought I had asked for vegetarian.
我當初有要求素食餐。

 I'm sorry. There are no more vegetarian meals.
對不起。已經沒有素食餐了。

 Then what kind of fish do you have?
那你們有什麼樣的魚？

Today we have *salmon* and pasta.
今天我們有鮭魚和義大利麵。

 I'll have the fish and a glass of white wine, please.
請給我魚和一杯白酒。

 Here you go. Enjoy your meal.
這是您的餐點。祝您用餐愉快。

 Thank you. It looks great.
謝謝。看起來很可口。

Dialog 3

主題 ▶ *Asking for help.*
要求幫忙。

 Excuse me. I hate to bother you, but I'm not feeling very well.

不好意思。我不想麻煩你，但是我覺得不太舒服。

 Oh no. What seems to be the matter?
喔，糟了。哪裡不舒服呢？

 I don't think the dinner is sitting very well with me.
我想我吃不慣之前的晚餐。

And to be honest, I'm not very good in airplanes.
而且，說實話，我不太習慣搭飛機。

We have some pills for *nausea*. Would you like to take that?

我們有一些暈機的藥片。您要不要吃一點？

Sure, anything to make this feeling go away.

好，只要能讓我舒服一點的東西都好。

All right. Let me get the pills and an *extra* blanket for you.

好的。我去拿藥片和多一條毛毯給您。

You'll feel better in no time.

您馬上就會覺得好多了。

Sentence Patterns　句型練習

I think we're all out of English papers.

我想，我們的英文報紙已經沒有了。

Oh, the usual: Business Week, Time and Newsweek...

喔，商業週刊、時代雜誌和新聞週刊……

I hate to bother you, but I'm not feeling very well.

我不想麻煩你，但是我覺得不太舒服。

And to be honest, I'm not very good in airplanes.

而且，說實話，我不太習慣搭飛機。

Vocabulary	字彙
☑ **first class**	頭等艙
☑ **upgrade**	升等
☑ **flight attendant**	空服員
☑ **upright**	立直的
☑ **nodded off**	打瞌睡
☑ **salmon**	鮭魚
☑ **nausea**	暈機
☑ **extra**	額外的

MEMO

Arriving
抵達目的地

Dialog 1

 主題 *Going through immigration.*
經過入境海關。

 Passport, please.
請拿出護照。

Here you go, sir.
先生，在這裡。

 Have you been to Taiwan before?
你以前到過台灣嗎？

No, I haven't. This is my first time.
沒有，我沒來過。這是我的第一次。

 How long do you plan to stay in Taiwan?
你計畫在台灣待多久？

Anywhere from ten to fourteen days. I'm not sure yet.
十天到十四天左右。我還不確定。

 You do realize that your visa is only valid for fourteen days, don't you?

你知道你的簽證有效期只有十四天，對吧？

Yes, I'm aware of that. I'll *reschedule* my flight in a few days.

是，這我知道。這幾天我就會重新安排我的回程飛機。

Very well then. Enjoy your trip to Taiwan.
那很好。祝你在台灣玩得愉快。

 Thank you very much.
非常謝謝你。

 Dialog 2

主題 *Asking for lost luggage.*
詢問遺失的行李。

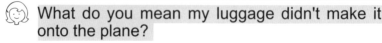 What do you mean my luggage didn't make it onto the plane?
你說我的行李不在飛機上是什麼意思？

How was that possible?
這怎麼可能？

 I'm sorry, madam.
小姐，我很抱歉。

But my computer says your luggage made it as far as Tokyo.
但是，我的電腦上顯示您的行李只運到東京。

It wasn't put onto the flight to Taipei.
它沒有被放上飛往台北的這班飛機。

 But what am I going to do? I've got everything in there.

但是，我要怎麼辦？我所有的東西都在裡面。

We can offer you a toiletries bag.
我們可以提供您一個盥洗用品袋。

 I don't want a toothbrush and comb! I want my bags!
我不需要牙刷和梳子！我要我的行李！

 I'm sorry. There's nothing I can do right now.
我很抱歉。目前，沒有我可以幫忙的地方。

When your luggage arrives, I will **contact** you at your hotel.
當您的行李抵達時，我會透過您的飯店聯絡您。

 Dialog 3

主題 *Exchanging money.*
換錢。

 Do you accept Canadian *traveler's checks*?
你們收加拿大的旅行支票嗎？

 Yes, but we have a 5% commission on traveler's *checks*.
收，但是我們兌換旅行支票收百分之五的佣金。

 That's a pretty *steep* fee.
那費用太高了。

Is the exchange rate for *notes* the same as for checks?
現金和支票的匯率是一樣的嗎？

Yes, they are. But there is no *commission* on cash.
是的，一樣。但是，兌換現金就不需要付佣金。

Very well then. I'll exchange C$200.
那好。我要換兩百元加幣。

Would you like that in large or small bills?
你要大面額還是小面額的紙鈔？

A bit of each would be nice.
都要。

Here is your money in Taiwan dollars. One thousand, two thousand...
這是兌換後的台幣。一千，兩千……

Sentence Patterns　句型練習

 It is very important to hang on to your luggage tags.
把你的行李標籤收好是很重要的。

 How long do you plan to stay in Taiwan?
你計畫在台灣待多久？

 You do realize that your visa is only valid for fourteen days, don't you?
你知道你的簽證有效期只有十四天，對吧？

What do you mean my luggage didn't make it onto the plane?

你說我的行李沒有放上飛機是什麼意思？

Vocabulary	字彙
☑ hang on	收好
☑ immigration	（入境）移民
☑ valid	有效的
☑ reschedule	重新安排
☑ contact	聯絡
☑ traveler's checks	旅行支票
☑ commission	佣金
☑ steep	過高的
☑ note	紙鈔

Welcome
歡迎

MP3-28

Dialog 1

 Welcoming someone at the airport.
在機場迎接某人。

Excuse me. Are you April Lee?
請問一下。你是艾波・李嗎？

You must be James. It's a pleasure to meet you.
你一定是詹姆士了。很榮幸認識你。

Likewise. Welcome to Taiwan. Did you have a pleasant flight?
我也是。歡迎到台灣。你旅途還愉快吧？

The movie was good but the food was terrible.
電影挺好看的，但是食物很糟。

Luckily, I had a good book to read.
幸好我有書可以看。

That's good. What do you want to do now?
那很好。你現在想要做什麼？

Should I take you to your hotel to rest?
我是不是應該帶你去飯店休息一下？

I'm a little bit *jet-lagged.* But I want to eat something first.
我有一點時差的問題。但是，我想先吃點東西。

126

I know just the place.
我知道一個地方不錯。

 Great. I'm *starving*!
太好了,我餓壞了。

 Dialog 2

主題 *Deciding what to eat.*
決定要吃什麼。

 What do you want to eat?
你想要吃什麼?

 I want to eat something light. I don't like to sleep on a full stomach.

我想吃點清淡的食物。我不要肚子漲漲地睡覺。

 This restaurant serves a very good beef noodle soup.

這家餐廳的牛肉麵湯不錯。

 It's too hot to have soup right now. I would prefer fried noodles.

現在天氣太熱了,沒辦法喝湯。我想吃炒麵好了。

 Yes, they have shrimp or *pork* fried noodles. Both are very delicious.

好,他們有蝦仁和豬肉炒麵。兩種都很好吃。

Great! Shrimp is my favorite.
太好了，我最喜歡蝦子了。

Dialog 3

 主題 *Saying good night.*
道晚安。

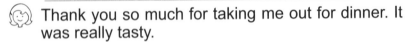 Thank you so much for taking me out for dinner. It was really tasty.
非常謝謝你招待我吃晚餐。它相當可口。

 I'm glad you enjoyed it. Here we are at the hotel.
我很高興你喜歡。飯店到了。

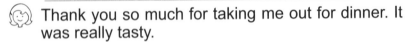 So what time can you *pick me up* tomorrow?
那你明天幾點來接我？

 Can you be ready at 10:00? We can go for a tour of the *factory*.
你十點可以準備好嗎？我們可以去參觀工廠。

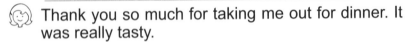 Ten am is fine. I'll wait for you in the *lobby*.
早上十點沒問題。我會在大廳等你。

 Sleep well. I'll see you in the morning.
好好睡一覺。我們明天早上見。

Sentence Patterns 句型練習

The movie was good but the food was terrible.
電影挺好看的，但是食物很糟。

Luckily, I had a good book to read.
幸好我有書可以看。

I would prefer fried noodles.
我想吃炒麵好了。

Here we are at the hotel.
飯店到了。

Vocabulary	字彙
☑ terminal	航站大廈
☑ jet-lagged	有時差問題的
☑ starving	很餓的
☑ pork	豬肉
☑ pick me up	接送我
☑ factory	工廠
☑ lobby	大廳

Checking in to a Hotel
辦理飯店住宿登記

🔘 MP3-29

Dialog 1

 Checking in at hotel reception.
在飯店櫃台辦理住宿登記。

Welcome to the Holiday Inn. How can I help you?
歡迎到假期飯店。我能幫您什麼忙嗎？

My name is April Lee. I'm *checking in.*
我的名字是艾波・李。我要辦理住宿登記。

Yes, Ms. Lee. We've been expecting you.
是的，李小姐。我們一直期待您的到來。

Can I have a room with a view?
我可以要一個有風景的房間嗎？

Do you want a single or *double bed*?
你要單人床還是雙人床。

A *double bed* will be more comfortable.
雙人床會比較舒服。

There's a room available on the 22nd floor. How about that?

在22樓有一間空房。您覺得如何？

That sounds good, as long as there are no earthquakes!

聽起來很好，只要沒有地震發生的話！

Dialog 2

主題 *Describing the hotel.*
描述這間飯店。

Have you stayed with us before?
你以前來這裡住宿過嗎？

No, I haven't. This is my first time to Taiwan.
沒有。這是我第一次到台灣來。

Well then, let me tell you about our hotel.
那好，讓我來介紹一下我們的飯店。

We have a swimming pool on the second floor.
我們在2樓有一個游泳池。

Is there an *exercise room*, too?
也有健身房嗎？

Yes, it's on the same floor. There's also a *rooftop* restaurant.
有，跟游泳池在同一層樓。在樓頂還有一家餐廳。

What time is it open for breakfast?
他們幾點開放用早餐？

It opens at 6:00 am every morning.
每天早上六點開門。

Perfect! Breakfast with a view!
太好了，一邊吃早餐還可以一邊看風景。

Dialog 3

Riding up the elevator.
搭電梯。

Can I help you with your bags?
我可以幫您提行李嗎?

Please. I think I *over-packed*.
麻煩你。我想我打包太多東西了。

How long will you be staying in Taiwan?
您會在台灣待多久?

About ten days. So, two big suitcases is a bit too much, isn't it?

大概十天左右。所以,兩個大箱子是有點太多,對吧?

Of course not. You need the space for souvenirs!
當然不會啦。你需要放紀念品的空間!

My thoughts exactly!
我也是這樣想的!

Here is your room and here's your key. Enjoy your stay.

這是您的房間和鑰匙。祝您住宿愉快。

Thank you, Gus. And here's a small tip for all your help.

謝謝你,葛斯。這是一點小費,謝謝你的幫忙。

Sentence Patterns 句型練習

We've been expecting you.
我們一直期待您的到來。

That sounds good, as long as there are no earthquakes!
聽起來很好，只要沒有地震發生的話！

My thoughts exactly!
我也是這樣想的！

And here's a small tip for all your help.
這是一點小費，謝謝你的幫忙。

Vocabulary 字彙

☐ checking in	住宿登記
☐ double bed	雙人床
☐ exercise room	健身房
☐ rooftop	屋頂
☐ elevator	電梯
☐ over-packed	打包太多東西的

UNIT 9 Breakfast in the Restaurant
在餐廳吃早餐

Dialog 1

 主題 *Asking for a table.*
要求用餐的桌子。

😄 Good morning. Table for one?
早安。一個人用餐？

😊 Yes. Non-smoking if you have it.
對，如果你們有禁煙區，請帶我到禁煙區。

😄 Of course. Right this way.
當然。這邊請。

😊 How about something by the window? The view is *spectacular*.
我可以坐在窗邊嗎？風景很漂亮。

😄 How about this one? You can see most of downtown from here.
這個位子如何？從這裡您可以看到大部分的市區。

😊 We're up so high. I'm getting *dizzy* already.
我們在這麼高的地方。我開始感到暈眩了。

😄 Then let's get something into your stomach. Here's your menu.
那趕快讓您吃點東西吧。這是菜單。

😊 Thank you. I'm famished.
謝謝。我餓壞了。

Dialog 2

 主題

Ordering breakfast.
點早餐

Do you have any *specials* today?
你們今天有什麼特餐嗎？

Yes, our breakfast special is *French toast* with strawberries.

有，我們的早點特餐是法國土司和新鮮草莓。

What does it come with?
搭配些什麼？

It comes with coffee and juice.
搭配咖啡及果汁。

That sounds perfect. Can I have orange juice please?

聽起來很棒。我可以點柳橙汁嗎？

Certainly. And how do you like your coffee?
當然。您的咖啡要加什麼嗎？

Two creams and one sugar please.
請加兩匙奶精和一匙糖。

One breakfast special coming up!
一份早點特餐馬上就來。

Dialog 3

主題 *Telling the waiter about the meal.*
反應餐點的問題。

How was your breakfast?
您的早餐如何？

It was good, but the strawberries were too *sour*.
很好，但是草莓太酸了。

Oh, I'm sorry. I'll tell the *chef*.
喔，我很抱歉。我會跟廚師說。

Don't worry about it. Besides that, everything else was sublime.
不用太擔心。除了那個之外，其他的都很棒。

I'm glad to hear it. Here's your bill.
很高興聽到您這麼說。這是您的帳單。

Please charge it to Room 2201.
請把帳記在2201號房。

Then can I have your *signature* on the bill please?
可以請您在帳單上簽名嗎？

No problem. Can I also leave you a tip by signing?
沒問題。我可以順便留小費給你嗎？

Of course! How can I say no to that?
那當然。我怎麼能說不可以？

Sentence Patterns 句型練習

🍎 Yes. Nonsmoking if you have it.
對，如果你們有禁煙區，請帶我到禁煙區。

🍎 Right this way.
這邊請。

🍎 Then let's get something into your stomach.
那趕快讓您吃點東西吧。

🍎 What does it come with?
搭配些什麼？

Vocabulary	字彙
☑ scrambled	（蛋）炒的
☑ sunny-side up	（蛋）單面煎的
☑ spectacular	壯麗的
☑ dizzy	暈眩的
☑ specials	特餐
☑ French toast	法國吐司
☑ sour	酸的
☑ signature	簽名

Checking Out
退房

Dialog 1

 Complaining about the room.
抱怨房間的設備。

Good morning. I'd like to *check out* of room 2201.
早安。我要辦理2201號房的退房事宜。

You're leaving us so soon?
您這麼快就要離開了？

Yes, I'm so excited. My friends and I are *heading down* the East Coast today.

是，我很興奮。今天我的朋友和我要到東海岸去。

That does sound exciting. And how was your stay here?

聽起來真令人興奮。那您在這裡住得還好嗎？

I hate to complain, but there's something definitely wrong with the shower.

我不喜歡抱怨，但是房間裡的淋浴設備一定有問題。

Really? What was the problem?
真的？是什麼問題？

The water kept changing from hot to cold, cold to hot.

水溫一直變，忽冷忽熱的。

I'm so sorry. I'll have someone look at it right away.
真抱歉。我會馬上找人去看看。

 Dialog 2

Making a suggestion.
給予建議。

 Besides the shower, was there any other problem?
除了淋浴設備外,還有其他問題嗎?

 No problems. But I'd like to make one suggestion.
沒有了。但是,我想提出一個建議。

I think you should keep the swimming pool open later.
我覺得你們應該將游泳池的開放時間延長。

 Actually, many guests have said the same thing.
事實上很多客人都反應過這件事。

Closing it at 8:00 pm is too early, isn't it?
晚上八點關閉,太早了一些,對吧?

 Well, by the time I get back from work the doors are already locked.
嗯,等我下班回來,門都已經關上了。

 Thanks for letting us know. I'll pass it onto my supervisor.
謝謝您告訴我們這件事。我會讓我的主管知道這件事。

Thanks. This is a nice place. I'd like to stay here the next time I'm in town.

謝了。這個地方不錯。我下次再來的時候，我會再來這裡住。

Dialog 3

主題

Processing a credit card.

處理刷卡事宜。

Did you use anything in the mini-bar?

您有使用小吧台裡的東西嗎？

Yes, I had two sodas and a bottle of beer.

有，我喝了兩瓶汽水和一瓶啤酒。

The computer says you also made two *long distance* phone calls.

電腦上顯示您打了兩通長途電話。

Right. Plus, I charged a couple of meals to my room too.

對。還有，我也將幾次餐點的帳單記在房間上了。

All together your bill comes to a total of NT$4500.

您的帳單全部總額為四千五百塊台幣。

Will that be cash or *plastic*?

你要用現金還是信用卡付帳？

I think my Visa is *maxed out*. Put it on my American Express instead.

我想我的Visa卡已經刷爆了。我想刷美國運通卡。

Gus processes the credit card.
葛斯處理信用卡的事宜。

 Here is your receipt.
這是您的收據。

Thank you very much for staying with us.
謝謝您在我們這裡住宿。

I hope you come again.
希望您下次再光臨。

 I sure will. See you next time.
我一定會的。下次見。

Sentence Patterns 句型練習

🍎 You're leaving us so soon?
您這麼快就要離開了？

🍎 I hate to complain, but there's something definitely wrong with the shower.
我不喜歡抱怨，但是淋浴設備一定有問題。

🍎 I think you should keep the swimming pool open later.
我想你們應該將游泳池的開放時間延長。

🍎 All together your bill comes to a total of NT$ 4500.

您的帳單全部加總是四千五百塊台幣。

Vocabulary	字彙
☑ ranked	排名
☑ service	服務
☑ check out	退房
☑ heading down	南下前往……
☑ processing	處理
☑ long distance	長途
☑ plastic	信用卡（口語說法）
☑ maxed out	（信用卡）刷爆的

4

Around the Island
環島

One of the best parts of visiting Taiwan is walking through the night markets. Most tourists make a point of visiting Huaxi Street and Shihlin Night Market.

It's a good idea to bargain when shopping for souvenirs. Depending on the country you're traveling in, the real price is much lower than the displayed price.

來台灣旅遊其中一項最好玩的活動莫過於逛夜市。大多數的遊客都不會錯過華西街和士林夜市。 買紀念品時，討價還價是項不錯的主意。視你所旅行的國家而定，通常貨品的實際價格都比標價上的要低很多。

UNIT 1

Renting a Car
租車

Dialog 1

 Asking to rent a car.
詢問租車事宜。

Hello. I would like to *rent* a car. Are there any available today?
哈囉！我想租輛車。請問今天還有車出租嗎？

We still have a few available.
我們還有一些車可以出租。

How many days do you need the car for?
您想要租幾天呢？

Let's see. I need it starting today for six days.
我想想看。從今天算的話我需要租六天。

We have a one-week *discount*. If you *rent* it for one full week, you will save 10%.
我們有提供一週租借的優惠。如果你租一星期的話，可以打九折。

That sounds good. I don't want to hurry.
聽起來不錯。我也不想趕。

You also get 700km free *mileage*. Additional kilometers will be NT$5 each.
而且可以獲得七百里數免付費。多出來每一公里五元。

Taiwan is not that big. I'm sure 700km will be enough.

台灣沒那麼大。七百公里絕對夠了。

All right then. Let's go out to the garage and pick out a car.

那好。我們去車庫選車吧。

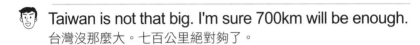

主題 *Discussing requirements for a car.*
討論車子配備。

What kind of car are you interested in? *Compact*, medium or full-sized?

您想租哪類型的車呢？小型，中型，加長型？

There will only be two of us. A *compact* car will be enough.

我們只有兩個人。小型車就夠了。

It's much easier to find parking for a small car.

小車也比較好找停車位。

And they don't use as much gas either.

而且也比較省油。

Yes, it will be much cheaper. But are you driving into the mountains?

是的，會比較省錢。但是你們會開上山嗎？

Yes, why?

會，有問題嗎？

 It may be cheaper, but you might have trouble *getting up* the mountains.

它可能比較便宜，但開山路可能有點困難。

 Good point. Then let's take a look at the medium-sized cars.

說的對。那我們去選一輛中型車吧。

 Dialog 3

主題 *Asking for a recommendation.*
要求推薦。

 We have two medium-sized vehicles available: a Ford or a Honda.

我們還有兩輛空的中型車。一台是福特，一台本田。

 I don't know very much about cars. Which one do you recommend?

我對車子沒什麼概念。你推薦哪一輛？

 I recommend the Honda. This is a very *reliable model*.

我建議你租本田。這台很可靠。

Why don't you get behind the wheel?

你何不試坐看看？

It's very comfortable. Does it have a CD player?
坐起來很舒適。有CD播放器嗎？

Yes, there is a CD player and air conditioning.
有的，CD播放器和冷氣都有。

I guess that's all I need for a comfortable drive.
嗯，我想這些就足以令我行車舒適了。

Should I complete the paperwork?
紙上作業就交給我了？

Sure. I need to get to the airport right away.
對。我得馬上趕到機場。

Sentence Patterns 句型練習

Are there any available today?
今天有車出租嗎？

It may be cheaper, but you might have trouble getting up the mountains.
它可能比較便宜，但開山路可能有點困難。

I recommend the Honda.
我建議你租本田。

Should I complete the paperwork?
紙上作業就交給我了？

Vocabulary	字彙
☑ renting	租
☑ discount	折扣
☑ mileage	總里數
☑ compact	小型的
☑ getting up	爬上（山路）
☑ reliable	可靠
☑ model	車型

MEMO

 MP3-33

Dialog 1

主題 *Discussing movies.*
討論電影。

🙂 What's your *favorite* movie?
你最喜歡哪部電影？

🙂 You mean my *favorite* movie *of all time*? That's a tough one.
你是說有史以來最喜歡的電影？真是個難題。

🙂 I'm partial to romances myself. My *favorite* movie is Titanic.
我偏好文藝片。我最喜歡的是「鐵達尼號」。

🙂 I don't mind romances, but I much prefer *action movies.*
文藝片對我來說還好，但我比較喜歡動作片。

🙂 Most guys like action movies, don't they?
大多數男生喜歡看動作片，對吧？

🙂 Well, I'm one of them. But to choose a *favorite* one is just impossible.
嗯，我就是其中之一。但是要選出最喜歡的一部就難了。

Dialog 2

主題 ▶ *Discussing exercise.*
討論運動。

 You look like you're in pretty good shape. Do you play any sports?
你看起來身材不錯。你有從事什麼運動嗎？

 No. I'm not very athletic at all. What about you?
沒有。我一點都不喜歡運動。你呢？

 I used to play basketball in university.
我大學時常打籃球。

Since then I haven't done much exercise.
但從那之後就很少運動。

 I know what you mean.
我瞭解。

I have to *force* myself to go to the *gym* a couple of times a week.
我也得強迫自己每週固定去健身房幾次。

 It's not easy to find time to exercise.
要找出時間運動不太容易。

Nowadays my only exercise is walking to the 7-11.
現在我唯一的運動就是步行到便利商店。

Well, that's better than nothing!
總比完全不運動來的好。

Dialog 3

主題 *Talking about the weather.*
討論天氣。

James, can you turn up the air-conditioning in this car?
詹姆士，你可以把車上的冷氣開強點嗎？

It's already on *full blast*, April.
這已經是最強的了。

Really? I'm still *sweating*.
真的嗎？可是我還在流汗。

I guess you're not used to hot weather.
我想你不習慣熱天氣。

My idea of a hot day is 25 degrees Celsius. Also, it's so *humid*!
我對熱天氣的定義是攝氏二十五度。而且，現在很潮濕！

Then I hope you have plenty of light clothing for this trip!
我希望這趟旅遊你帶了很多輕薄的衣物。

Sentence Patterns 句型練習

I'm partial to romances myself.
我偏好文藝片。

I don't mind romances, but I much prefer action movies.
我不介意看文藝片，但是我比較喜歡動作片。

I'm not very athletic at all.
我一點都不喜歡運動。

Since then I haven't done much exercise.
從那之後我就很少運動。

Vocabulary	字彙
☑ favorite	最喜歡
☑ of all time	有史以來
☑ action movie	動作片
☑ force	力量
☑ gym	健身房
☑ full blast	最強的
☑ sweating	正在流汗的
☑ humid	潮濕的

Hiking at Taroko Gorge
太魯閣健行之旅

Dialog 1

Preparing things for a hike.
準備徒步旅行的裝備。

Let's see. We've got snacks, sunglasses and extra film.
我看看。我們有點心，太陽眼鏡和備用底片。

Anything else we need for this hike?
健行還要帶什麼嗎？

Some parts of the *trail* are pretty *slippery*. Do you have good shoes?
有些路段很滑。你有好的鞋子嗎？

All I have are these sports sandals. Will they do?
我只有這些運動涼鞋。這些行嗎？

They should be fine. It's pretty hot today so don't forget your sun cream.
應該可以。今天很熱，所以不要忘記帶防曬乳液。

Good idea. I get *sunburned* very easily. And one last thing: water.
好主意。我很容易曬傷。最後一樣東西：水。

Right. There are no 7-11s on the way.
沒錯。沿途沒有便利商店。

Dialog 2

 主題 *Starting a hike.*
開始徒步旅行。

How long is this hike?
這段路有多長？

It's 12 km *round trip*. It should take us about three hours.

來回共十二公里。大約要三小時才走的完。

Three hours if I don't hold you back. Remember, I'm really out of shape.

三小時，如果我沒有拖慢你的話。我體力不好，記得吧。

Oh, don't worry. We can go slowly and enjoy the *scenery*.

喔，別擔心。我們可以慢慢走欣賞風景。

It's really breathtaking, isn't it? I've never seen such beautiful *cliffs*.

真是令人嘆為觀止，對吧？我從來沒看過這麼美的峭壁。

I couldn't agree more. What's more, this *trail* goes all the way to a *waterfall*.

我再同意不過了。除此之外，這條路會直通到瀑布。

Really? I can't wait!
真的嗎？我等不及了。

Then let's get going!
那我們走吧！

Dialog 3

Enjoying the end of the hike.
快樂抵達。

 Are we there yet? I feel like we've walked for at least three hours already.

我們到了沒？我覺得我們最少已經走了三小時了。

Ⓜ️ We're almost there. Can't you hear the sound of rushing water?

我們快到了。你沒聽到水流聲嗎？

Ⓜ️ Yes, I can. Oh! There's the *waterfall* ! We're here at last.

嗯，有聽到。喔！瀑布在那裡。我們終於到了。

Ⓜ️ That's stunning, isn't it?
很令人震驚，是吧？

Ⓜ️ It's such a peaceful little spot.
真是平靜的好地方。

Ⓜ️ Do you want to jump in?
你想跳下水嗎？

Why not? Let's go for a *dip*.
有什麼不可以？我們下去泡泡水吧。

OK. Last one in is a rotten egg!
好。最後一個是笨蛋。

Sentence Patterns 句型練習

All I have are these sports sandals.
我只有這些運動涼鞋。

Will they do?
這些行嗎？

What's more, this *trail* goes all the way to a *waterfall*.
除此之外，這條路會直通到瀑布。

Last one in is a rotten egg!
最後一個是笨蛋！

Vocabulary 字彙

☑ hiking	健行
☑ trail	徒步道路
☑ slippery	滑的
☑ sunburned	被曬傷的
☑ round trip	來回旅程
☑ scenery	風景
☑ waterfall	瀑布
☑ dip	浸；泡

At the Night Market
逛夜市

Dialog 1

 Discussing night markets.
討論夜市。

I can't believe my eyes! There are so many people here!

我不敢相信我所看到的！這裡好多人喔！

Yes, the night markets in Taiwan are very *lively* places.

是的。在台灣，夜市是很熱鬧的地方。

I'll say! This is the biggest *crowd* I've seen since the U2 concert.

我同意。這是自U2演唱會以來，我所看到最多的人了。

People like to come out at night when it's not so hot.

大家都喜歡在晚上天涼時出門逛逛。

What do you think? Are you enjoying the *sights and sounds* of the night market?

你覺得呢？你喜歡夜市的景象和聲音嗎？

Yes, but I'm not sure I like the smell. What exactly is that?

是的。但是我不確定我喜歡那種味道。那到底是什麼味道？

Oh, that's our first snack't stinky tofu!

喔，那是我們第一個點心：臭豆腐！

Dialog 2

 主題 *Asking if someone has ever eaten something.*
詢問別人是否吃過某樣小吃。

Have you ever tried stinky tofu?
你吃過臭豆腐嗎？

I've had tofu before in a Chinese restaurant.
我以前在中國餐廳吃過豆腐。

Oh, that's not the same. Stinky tofu is a local *specialty*.

喔，那不一樣。臭豆腐是本地才有的特產。

I can't say it sounds very appetizing. Nor does it smell very good.

我不敢說它聽起來很好吃。聞起來也不怎麼樣。

Trust me. It tastes better than it smells. Should I get us a couple?

相信我。它吃起來比聞起來好吃多了。我要點兩份嗎？

All right. I'll try anything once. Get me a stinky tofu!
好吧。我什麼都嘗一次。給我一份臭豆腐。

Dialog 3

Eating dessert.
吃點心。

How about some ice cream for dessert?
點心要來點冰淇淋嗎？

Oh, I couldn't. I'm stuffed. Besides, I'm trying to lose some weight.

喔，我吃不下了。我撐死了。而且，我正在減肥。

But this shop sells really good ice cream. It's *homemade*.

但是這家店的冰淇淋真的很棒。是手工的哦 。

Hmm...What flavors do they have?
嗯……有什麼口味？

Let's see. They've got chocolate, peanut, and mango.

我看看。他們有巧克力、花生，和芒果。

Well, you don't have to *twist my arm*. I love mango!
好吧，你不用逼我。我喜歡吃芒果！

Two mango ice cream cones coming up!
兩份芒果冰淇淋甜筒來了！

(Sigh!) There goes my diet!
（唉）我的節食計畫泡湯了！

Sentence Patterns 句型練習

I can't believe my eyes!
我真不敢相信我所看到的！

I can't say it sounds very appetizing.
我不敢說它聽起來很好吃。

Besides, I'm trying to lose some weight.
而且，我正在減肥。

There goes my diet!
我的節食計畫泡湯了！

Vocabulary	字彙
☑ make a point	特別指定
☑ lively	生動
☑ crowd	人群
☑ sights and sounds	聲光景色
☑ specialty	特有的
☑ dessert	點心
☑ homemade	自製的
☑ twist my arm	逼我

In Traffic
交通

Dialog 1

 Asking about driving laws.
詢問駕駛規則。

What's the *speed limit* here?
這裡限速多少？

On this road it's 70km/hour. But *up ahead* we have to slow down.
這條路限時速七十。但是再過去一點就要開慢一點了。

I noticed that everyone else is slowing down too.
我也注意到大家都慢下來了。

Because everyone knows that there's a speed trap coming up.
因為大家都知道馬上就有測速照相機。

Oh! I saw the flash. The camera's hidden inside that box on the side of the road.
喔！我看到閃光燈了。照相機藏在路旁的箱子裡。

I sure hope that it didn't take a picture of us.
我希望我們沒被照到。

Dialog 2

 主題 *Asking about driving customs.*
詢問開車慣例。

How old do you have to be to drive in Canada?
在加拿大幾歲才能開車？

It depends on where you live. Usually you can start driving at 16.
那要看你住在哪裡。通常十六歲就可以開車了。

That's pretty young. Do you have to pass a test?
那很年輕耶。你們需要通過考試嗎？

Yes, but it's pretty easy.
是的，但是考的很簡單。

Many people also take a driving course to learn how to drive *properly*.
許多人會去上駕駛訓練課程，學習如何開好車。

This guy in front of me sure didn't take that course.
我前面那個人肯定沒上過類似的課。

Look at him! He's taking up the entire road!
看看他！他佔了整條路。

Maybe you can pass him.
也許你可以超他車。

There are no cars coming. Here's your chance. Go!
目前沒其它車開過來。快，現在是個好機會。

Dialog 3

 主題 *Complaining about traffic.*
抱怨交通路況。

The traffic in the countryside is so much better than in Taipei.

郊外的交通狀況比台北好太多了。

It sure is. Sometimes I'm stuck for hours on the *freeway*.

一點也沒錯。 有時候連在高速公路上都會塞上幾小時。

Maybe you can take the MRT instead.
也許你可以改搭捷運。

I do sometimes.
我有時候會。

Actually, the problem is not the traffic, but finding a parking spot.
事實上，交通不是問題，停車才是個大問題。

I can imagine it's quite difficult to find parking downtown.
我可以瞭解在市中心找停車位是多麼的困難。

It's pretty much impossible, unless you want to *pay an arm and a leg.*

幾乎是不太可能，除非你準備花大錢付費停車。

Sentence Patterns 句型練習

I noticed that everyone else is slowing down too.

我注意到大家都慢下來了。

It depends on where you live.

那要看你住在哪裡。

Maybe you can take the MRT instead.

也許你可以改搭捷運。

I can imagine it's quite difficult to find parking downtown.

我可以瞭解在市中心找停車位是多麼的困難。

Vocabulary	字彙
☑ traffic jams	交通阻塞
☑ rush hour	尖峰時段
☑ stuck in traffic	塞車
☑ speed limit	限速
☑ up ahead	前方
☑ properly	恰當地
☑ freeway	高速公路
☑ pay an arm and a leg	花大錢付費

MEMO

....
....
....
....
....
....

Going to the Beach
去海邊

🔘 MP3-37

Dialog 1

 主題 ▶ *Asking for directions.*
問路。

Can you recommend a nice beach near here?
你可以推薦這附近的漂亮海灘嗎？

There's a pleasant little beach on the *outskirts* of town.
在郊區那有一處不錯的小海灘。

Just keep going straight and you'll find it.
直走就可以找到了。

Is it busy? We're looking for something far away from the *crowds*.
那會很擁擠嗎？我們想找一處遠離人群的地方。

It's usually only busy on the weekends. You shouldn't have any problems today.
那裡通常只有週末才會有人潮。今天去應該不會有這個問題。

That sounds perfect. Straight ahead you say?
聽起來不錯。你剛是說直走嗎？

That's right. You'll see it on your right hand side.
沒錯。就在你的右手邊。

Dialog 2

 主題 *Going for a walk along the shore.*
沿岸漫步。

Do you want to go for a *stroll* along the shore?
你想去海岸邊散步嗎？

Sure. There are some beautiful rocks and *cliffs* to look at.
好啊。那有許多美麗的岩石和峭壁可看。

Look at these ones over here.
看看那邊那一些。

They look like they're from the age of the dinosaurs!
看起來好像從恐龍時代就有了。

Check this out. This rock even has a *fossil*.
看看這個。這個岩石居然還有化石。

I think this island must have been underwater millions of years ago.
我覺得這座島在幾百萬年前一定在海底。

Hmmm...wonder where we'll be a million years from now.
嗯⋯⋯真不知道一百萬年後我們會在哪。

Dialog 3

 主題 *Sun tanning on the beach.*
海邊日光浴。

This is the life, isn't it? Fresh air, sand, surf...
這才叫人生，對吧？新鮮空氣，沙灘，海浪……

It sure is. We couldn't have picked a better day to get a little sun.
的確是。再也沒有比今天更好的日子來曬太陽了。

Hey, do you want to try *surfing*?
嘿，想不想試試衝浪？

Actually, I'm not such a strong swimmer. I don't think I would enjoy *surfing*.
事實上，我對游泳不太行。我不認為我會喜歡衝浪。

Then how about just playing in the waves?
那在水上玩玩如何？

The sea *breeze* is making me a little sleepy.
海風吹的我有點睏。

That I can do. I'll race you to the water! Three-two-one, go!
可以。我們比賽看誰先跑到水裡！三，二，一，跑！

Sentence Patterns 句型練習

Straight ahead you say?
你剛是說直走嗎？

Check this out.
看看這個。

I wonder where we'll be a million years from now.
不知道一百萬年後我們會在哪。

We couldn't have picked a better day to get a little sun.
再也沒有比今天更好的日子來曬太陽了。

Vocabulary	字彙
☑ tan	曬成棕色
☑ outskirts	郊區
☑ stroll	漫步
☑ cliff	峭壁
☑ fossil	化石
☑ surfing	衝浪
☑ breeze	微風

MP3-38

Dialog 1

主題 ▶ *Taking a break.*
休息時間。

James, let's *take a break* at that roadside café.
詹姆士，我們在路旁的咖啡廳休息一下。

I wouldn't mind a coffee.
來杯咖啡也不錯。

I could use one too. My *eyelids* are getting heavy from driving all morning.

我也想來一杯。開了一早的車，我的眼皮都快撐不開了。

Why didn't you tell me? I can help drive too.
你怎沒都沒告訴我呢？我可以幫你開啊。

Why don't you take over after our break?
休息過後再換你吧？

It's a deal. I love driving through the mountains.
就這麼説定了。我喜歡開山路。

And I could use a nap.
我則可以小睡一下。

Dialog 2

主題 ▶ *Ordering coffee.*
點咖啡。

 Are you ready to order?
你準備要點餐了嗎？

 We'll just have a couple of coffees, please.
請給我們兩杯咖啡，謝謝。

 We have the house coffee which is made from Indonesian beans.

我們的招牌咖啡是印尼豆煮出來的。

We also have *lattes, cappuccinos, espresso...* you name it, we've got it.
也有拿鐵、卡布奇諾、濃縮咖啡……你說的出來的我們都有。

 That sure is a lot of choice.
果然有很多選擇。

Then we'll just have one *latte* and one house coffee, please.
那請給我們一杯拿鐵和一杯招牌咖啡。

 How about a snack?
需要來點點心嗎？

We have cheesecake with strawberries, raspberries, blueberries...

我們的起司蛋糕有草莓、覆盆子、藍莓口味⋯⋯

I get the picture. Two coffees will do for now, thanks.

我大概瞭解了。先點兩杯咖啡就好了，謝謝。

Dialog 3

 Discussing habits.

討論生活習慣。

Are you a big coffee drinker, April?

艾波，你喝咖啡喝得很兇嗎？

Only once in a while when I need a *pick-me-up*. I usually just drink tea.

偶爾當我需要提神時才喝。我通常喝茶。

Me, I need at least one cup in the morning to get me going.

我呢，早上至少要喝一杯以保持一天的清醒。

It's a bad *habit*, I know.

我知道這個習慣不好。

Drinking coffee isn't bad. There are plenty of worse things to be *addicted* to.

喝咖啡不會不好啊。對很多其它東西上癮更糟糕。

I guess you're right. I suppose it's better than smoking or gambling.

你說的沒錯。我認為那比抽煙或賭博好多了。

So don't worry. Drinking a coffee in the morning isn't going to ruin your life.

所以別擔心。早上喝一杯咖啡不會毀了你的人生的。

Sentence Patterns 句型練習

I wouldn't mind a coffee.
來杯咖啡也不錯。

It's a deal.
就這麼說定了。

I get the picture.
我大概瞭解了。

Me, I need at least one cup in the morning to get me going.
我呢，早上至少要喝一杯以保持一天的清醒。

Vocabulary	字彙
☑ centuries	幾世紀
☑ take a break	休息一下
☑ eyelids	眼皮
☑ latte	拿鐵
☑ cappuccino	卡布奇諾
☑ espresso	濃縮咖啡
☑ pick-me-up	提神
☑ habit	習慣
☑ addicted	上癮的

MEMO

At a Teahouse
在茶藝館

Dialog 1

 Discussing plans for the evening.
討論下午的計畫。

It's been a pretty long day. Should we just head back to the **bed and breakfast**?
今天夠累了。我們該直接回旅館去嗎？

I'm not ready to **hit the hay** yet. But I don't have enough energy for a bar.
我還沒打算上床睡覺。但是也沒力氣去酒吧玩。

Me neither. Besides, bars are much too smoky.
我也沒有。而且，酒吧內烏煙瘴氣的。

Would you be interested in going to a teahouse?
你想去茶藝館嗎？

I've heard wonderful things about Taiwanese tea.
我對台灣茶慕名已久。

I'd be very interested in going.
我很想去看看。

Let me check in my travel book. Maybe they recommend a good place for tea.
讓我查看一下旅遊書。他們也許有推薦喝茶的好地方。

Dialog 2

 主題

Ordering tea.
點茶。

I really like the *atmosphere* in here. It's so *mellow*.
我很喜歡這裡的氣氛。茶也很香醇。

Yes, it's very *cozy*. Here's the list of teas they have. What do you feel like?
是的，這裡很舒適。這裡有茶單。你想喝什麼？

I wouldn't even know where to start. The teas I'm used to come in bags!
我根本不知道點什麼好。我通常都喝茶包。

There's Oolong Tea, Te Guan Yin, Pu Erh...
有烏龍茶、鐵觀音、普洱等……。

Why don't we try something local?
我們點些當地的吧。

I heard there are excellent teas from these mountains.
我聽說這個山區出產的茶很棒。

Alright. Let's order some High Mountain Oolong tea. It's world famous.
好吧。我們點些高山烏龍茶。它是世界有名的。

Sure. I'll have a cup.
當然，我要來一杯。

 Actually, you'll have more than a cup.
事實上，人家不會只給你一杯的。

 Making tea.
泡茶。

 Making tea looks quite complicated.
泡茶看起來好複雜。

 Actually, it's pretty easy. I'll show you. First, fill the teapot with tea leaves.

實際上，它是非常簡單的。我示範給你看。首先，把茶葉放入茶壺裡。

 Ok. And now I'll pour in hot water, right?
好了。現在我要倒入熱水，對吧？

 Right. And when it's ready, just pour the tea into our cups.

是的。當好了呢，再把茶倒入杯子裡。

But don't drink it!
但是還先不要喝。

Don't drink it? What am I supposed to do if I don't drink it?

不能喝？不喝的話要做什麼？

 Just smell it.

先聞。

 Wow! That does smell good.

哇！聞起來還真香。

 Now do it again. And this time we can drink it.

再聞一次。然後這次就可以喝了。

Sentence Patterns　句型練習

🍎 Would you be interested in going to a teahouse?

你會想去茶藝館嗎？

🍎 I wouldn't even know where to start.

我根本不知道怎麼開始。

🍎 Making tea looks quite complicated.

泡茶看起來好複雜。

🍎 First, fill the teapot with tea leaves.

首先，把茶葉放入茶壺裡。

Vocabulary	字彙
☑ discovered	發現
☑ bed and breakfast	供宿和早餐的旅館
☑ hit the hay	去睡覺
☑ atmosphere	氣氛
☑ mellow	香醇的
☑ cozy	舒適的
☑ teapot	茶壺

M E M O

In a Temple
在廟裡

Dialog 1

 主題 *Taking photos of a temple.*
廟宇拍照。

Hey, let's stop up ahead. I know of a cool little *temple*.

嘿，我們在前面停一下。我知道那有一座不錯的小廟。

Sure, I wouldn't mind taking a few photographs of it. I hope that's allowed.

當然，我們拍幾張照吧。希望可以拍照。

Sure, why not? Just be *considerate* of people praying.

當然，為何不？不要打擾到拜拜的人就好了。

Of course. I'm always careful not to disturb others.

當然。我會很小心不打擾到別人的。

Besides, can you imagine any of these *monks* getting angry at you?

而且你能想像這些和尚對你生氣的樣子嗎？

Definitely not. They look so kind and happy.

當然不能。他們看起來很慈悲又喜樂。

Dialog 2

 Discussing religion.
討論宗教。

😊 Are most people in Taiwan Buddhist?

大多數台灣人都信佛教嗎？

😀 Most are either Buddhist or Taoist. What about in Canada?

大多數不是佛教就是道教。在加拿大呢？

😊 Most Canadians are Christian, but there are plenty of other *religions* too.

大多數加拿大人信基督教，但是也有很多其它信仰。

😀 I hope you don't mind me asking, but are you Christian?

我希望你不介意我問，你是基督徒嗎？

😊 I was brought up Christian. But I guess I'm not a practicing Christian.

我從小就信基督了。但是我不算很虔誠。

😀 I heard that nowadays many young people don't follow *traditional religions*.

我聽說現在很多年輕人並沒完全遵循傳統宗教。

That's true. We're too busy making money to go to church.

沒錯。我們忙著賺錢而沒有時間上教堂。

Yes. And our God is money!

是的，錢就是我們的上帝。

Dialog 3

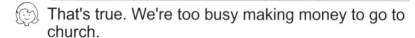

主題 *Talking about things in a temple.*

談論廟裡的東西。

Hey, April! Come check this out.

嘿，艾波！ 來看看這個。

That's an amazing statue. She must have a million eyes and a million arms.

這座雕像真是不可思議。她一定有千眼千手。

Yes, that's Kuan-Yin. She's a Buddhist *deity*.

是的，那是觀音。祂是佛教的神明。

Why does she have so many arms and eyes?

為何祂有那麼多手和眼睛呢？

Well, sometimes she only has two or four arms and eyes.

嗯，有時候祂只有二到四個手眼。

But it just means that she is extremely kind.
不過那些都只是象徵祂慈悲無量。

Let me guess. The eyes mean that she can see other people's pain.

我猜猜看。眼睛代表祂能看到別人的苦難。

And the arms mean she tries to help. Right?
而手則代表祂想伸出援手，是吧？

Exactly. It's something that many Buddhists try to be.

一點都沒錯。而那也是許多佛教信徒想做到的。

Well, you don't have to be Buddhist to believe in that!

嗯，但是你不一定要是佛教徒才會去信奉那些觀念。

Sentence Patterns　句型練習

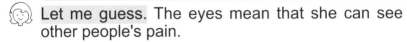I'm always careful not to disturb others.
我會很小心不打擾到別人的。

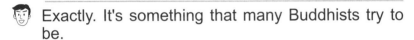I hope you don't mind me asking, but are you Christian?
我希望你不介意我問，你是基督徒嗎？

I was brought up Christian.
我從小就信基督了。

Let me guess.
讓我猜猜。

Vocabulary	字彙
☑ monk	和尚
☑ nun	尼姑
☑ vow	誓約
☑ temple	廟宇
☑ considerate	為人著想的;體貼的
☑ religion	宗教
☑ traditional	傳統的
☑ deity	神明

MEMO

Shopping for Souvenirs

買紀念品

MP3-41

 Dialog **1**

主題 *Asking about a statue.*
詢問雕像。

Welcome to The *Marble* Collection.
歡迎光臨大理石雕塑。

Please let me know how I can help you.
請問有什麼需要嗎？

Sure. Tell me about this marble statue.
是的。請介紹一下這座大理石雕像。

Ah...that's one of my favorites. It's Kuan-Yin.
啊！那是我的最愛之一。那是觀音。

Yes, I know. I've seen her before.
對，我知道。我之前看過。

This one is even more beautiful than the one I saw
at the temple.
這尊比我之前在廟裡看到的還漂亮。

She is hand made. Just take a look at how
detailed it is.
這尊是純手工製的。請仔細看雕工很細。

How long does it take to make it?
做這一尊要多久時間？

I can't be certain. But most statues take almost two months to *create*.
我不確定。但是大多數雕像要花上近兩個月的時間。

No wonder it's so beautiful!
難怪它那麼漂亮。

Dialog 2

主題 *Bargaining with a shopkeeper.*
和老闆殺價。

How much do you want for this statue?
這尊雕像你要賣多少？

It's NT$10,000.
一萬元。

What? That's way too expensive!
什麼？那太貴了吧！

But just think of the work that went into it.
想想它是花多少心力去雕刻。

You can't buy a statue like this in your home country.
你在你的國家買不到這樣的雕像。

True, but it's still overpriced. How about a discount?
沒錯，但是還是太貴了。打個折如何？

I can give you 15% off. But that's it.
我可以給你八五折。但就只能這樣了。

Make it 20% and you've got a deal.
八折就成交。

You *drive a hard bargain*. 20% off it is. You've got a deal.

你很會殺價。打八折。就這麼說定了。

Dialog 3

主題 *Sending a parcel home.*
寄包裹回家。

Now the problem is taking it home. It's quite heavy.
現在的問題是要怎麼拿回家。滿重的。

I can package it and send it by mail.
我可以打包然後郵寄。

Yes, but I wonder if that's safe. I'd hate to have it *damaged*.

可以，但是我又擔心安不安全。我不希望它損傷。

We post packages all the time with no problems.
我們每次寄都沒發生過問題。

What if it gets lost? Is there a warranty?
如果遺失了呢？ 會有保障嗎？

You can buy insurance in case it gets lost.
你擔心遺失的話可以買保險。

But this hasn't happened to us before.
不過這種事從未發生過。

All right then. Just put some extra newspapers in the box.
那好吧。放些報紙在盒子裡吧。

It will give me *peace of mind*.
那樣我會覺得安心點。

No problem. You'll meet up with Kuan-Yin again in 3 weeks.
沒問題。三星期後，你就會與這尊觀音相見啦。

Sentence Patterns 句型練習

I can't be certain.
我不確定。

How much do you want for this statue?
這尊雕像你要賣多少？

True, but it's still overpriced.
沒錯，但那還是太貴了！

You can buy insurance in case it gets lost.
你擔心遺失的話可以買保險。

Vocabulary	字彙
☑ bargain	殺價
☑ marble	大理石
☑ detailed	精細的
☑ create	創造
☑ drive a hard bargain	很會殺價
☑ damaged	損傷
☑ peace of mind	安心

5

Out on the Town
出城去

One of the best things about living in the city is getting out of the city. On the weekends many people like to go into the countryside for a picnic or barbecue.

A pub is a bar where you can have a drink and something small to eat. A club, on the other hand, is a bar where you can dance the night away. Clubs usually have a ***bouncer*** at the door who checks your ID and collects a cover charge.

住在城裡最有趣的活動之一便是出城。週末很多都市人會喜歡去郊外野餐或烤肉。酒吧是一個你可以喝酒、吃一點東西的店。另一方面，俱樂部則是你可以徹夜跳舞的地方。通常俱樂部的門口會有彪形大漢檢查你的身份證明並收取入場費用。

MP3-42

主題 *Asking someone to a movie.*
邀請人去看電影。

Do you want to catch a flick?
你要去看電影嗎？

Why not? There's nothing on TV tonight.
好啊。反正今晚也沒什麼電視節目。

Let's check out Charlie's Angels 2. It's the latest *Hollywood blockbuster*.

我們去看「霹靂嬌娃」第二集。它是好萊塢最近的當紅炸子雞。

But I usually don't like to watch *sequels*.
但是我通常不喜歡看續集。

They're never as good as the *original* movie.
他們從未比第一集好。

But I heard this one is not bad.
但我聽說這部還不錯。

Besides, don't you want to watch three beautiful women?
再說，難道你不想看三位美女嗎？

Since you put it that way, how could I refuse?
既然你都那樣說了，我怎能拒絕呢？

Dialog 2

 Buying movie tickets.
買電影票。

Two tickets for the 9:00 show, please.
請給我兩張九點的票。

I'm sorry. The 9:00 showing is *sold out*.
抱歉。九點的票賣光了。

There are tickets available for the 9:30 and 10:00 shows.
現在只剩九點半和十點場次的票。

Are there still good seats left for 9:30?
九點半那場還有好座位嗎？

Actually, most of the good seats are already taken.
事實上，大部分的好座位都滿了。

You should wait for the 10:00 show.
你應該等十點那場。

Then I'll take two tickets for the 10:00 show.
那我買兩張十點的票。

That's one adult and one student ticket, please.
一張成人，一張學生，謝謝。

 That comes to NT$350, please.
總共三百五十元，謝謝。

Dialog 3

 Buying popcorn.
買爆米花。

We've got a few minutes left before the show.
還有幾分鐘才開演。

Yeah, just enough time to *line up* for some popcorn.
是的。時間剛好夠排隊買爆米花。

Wow! Just look at those prices.
哇！看看價位！

No kidding. It's not worth it to just buy popcorn.
不是真的吧。只買爆米花划不來。

There's more *value* if you buy one of the combos.
買套餐比較划算。

The combo *includes* a drink and a chocolate bar.
套餐附一杯飲料和一根巧克力棒。

That sounds good. We can share.
聽起來不錯。我們可以一起分。

Sentence Patterns 句型練習

Do you want to catch a flick?
你要去看電影嗎？

Since you put it that way, how could I refuse?
既然你都那樣說了，我怎能拒絕呢？

That comes to NT$350, please.
總共三百五十元，謝謝。

It's not worth it to just buy popcorn.
只買爆米花划不來。

Vocabulary 字彙

☑ upcoming	即將來臨的
☑ Hollywood blockbuster	好萊塢強片
☑ sequel	續集
☑ original	原來的
☑ sold out	賣光的
☑ line up	排隊
☑ value	價值
☑ include	包含

Going Out for Lunch

外出中餐

MP3-43

Dialog 1

 Deciding where to go for lunch.
討論午餐地點。

Where do you want to go for lunch?
中餐想去哪裡吃？

I don't know. What are you in the mood for?
我不知道。你有主意嗎？

How about the Italian restaurant down the street?
街上那家義大利餐廳如何？

No, I just had *pasta* last night.
不要。我昨晚才吃過通心麵。

Oh, I know. There's that new steakhouse on the corner.

喔，我知道。街角有家新開的牛排館。

That sounds good. I walked by it last night. It smelled really great.

聽起來不錯。我昨晚有經過，聞起來很棒。

Dialog 2

主題 ▶ *Ordering steak.*
點牛排。

 Have you decided?
請問您決定了嗎？

 Not yet. What's the difference between the Sirloin Steak and the House Steak?

還沒。請問沙朗牛排和招牌牛排有何不同？

 The House steak has *mushrooms* and *gravy* on top. The Sirloin doesn't.

招牌牛排有磨菇和肉汁。沙朗牛排沒有。

 Hmmm...I'm not a fan of mushrooms. I'll have the Sirloin, please.

嗯。我不喜歡磨菇。請給我一份沙朗牛排。

 And how would you like that done?
請問要幾分熟？

 Medium-rare please. Please make sure the *chef* doesn't overcook it.

三分熟，謝謝。請跟廚師說不要煮過熟。

Dialog 3

主題 ▶ *Ordering a starter.*
點前菜。

What's the *soup of the day*?
今日例湯是什麼？

Today we have Cream of Corn.
今天我們有奶油玉米濃湯。

Sure, I'll have a bowl of soup. And what else does my steak come with?

好，那我要一碗。我的牛排餐還附什麼？

The steak comes with French Fries and a salad.
牛排餐還附薯條和沙拉。

What kind of *salad dressing* would you like?
你想要什麼口味的沙拉調味醬？

What kinds do you have?
你們有什麼？

We have French, Italian and Thousand Island Dressings.

我們有法式、義大利式調味醬和千島醬。

I'll have the French, please.
請給我法式調味醬。

Very well. I'll bring your soup out first.
很好。我會先端湯給你。

Sentence Patterns 句型練習

What are you in the mood for?
你有主意嗎？

What's the difference between the Sirloin Steak and the House Steak?
請問沙朗牛排和招牌牛排有何不同？

I'm not a fan of mushrooms.
我不喜歡磨菇。

The steak comes with French Fries and a salad.
牛排餐還附薯條和沙拉。

Vocabulary	字彙
☑ **rare**	生的
☑ **pasta**	通心麵
☑ **mushrooms**	磨菇
☑ **gravy**	肉湯汁
☑ **chef**	主廚
☑ **soup of the day**	每日特湯
☑ **salad dressing**	沙拉調味醬

Going Out for Dinner

外出晚餐

主題 *Deciding on an appetizer.*
點開胃菜。

This is such a nice restaurant. Can we afford it?
這家餐廳真不錯。我們付的起嗎？

Oh, don't worry. Let's just *splurge* a little!
喔，別擔心。我們奢侈一下吧。

All right. Do you want to share an *appetizer*?
好吧。你要一起分開胃菜嗎？

Sure. I'm ok with the chicken wings or the veggie platter.
好啊。雞翅和青菜拼盤都不錯。

Let's go with the chicken wings. I'm in the mood for something spicy.
我們選雞翅吧。我想吃點辛辣的。

Good choice. I love spicy food, too.
好主意。我也喜歡辣的。

Dialog 2

主題 *Ordering a drink from the bar.*
在酒吧裡點飲料。

Can I get you something from the bar?
請問要點些什麼？

Do you have a wine list?
你有酒單嗎？

Here you are, madam.
這裡，小姐。

What's your *house red?*
你們店裡是哪種紅酒？

Our house red is a Chilean Merlot. Our house white is from France.
我們的紅酒是智利馬龍。白酒是法國的。

Can you recommend a heavier red wine?
可以推薦烈一點的紅酒嗎？

I would recommend a bottle of Italian Chianti. It's one of our best.
我推薦您義大利的吉安帝酒。那是我們店裡最好的酒之一。

That sounds good. We'll have a bottle of Chianti.
聽起來不錯。來瓶吉安帝吧。

Dialog 3

主題 ▶ *Deciding a tip.*
決定小費。

Well, I'm just stuffed. I've never eaten so much in my life.
我撐死了。我這輩子沒吃那麼多過。

Me neither. Everything was so delicious.
我也沒有。每樣都好美味。

And the service here was so good. Should we leave the waiter a tip?
服務也很好。我們要給服務生小費嗎？

The *service charge* should already be included in the bill.
服務費應該已經加在帳單裡了。

You're right. There's a 10% service charge.
沒錯。百分之十的服務費。

Hey, should we *go Dutch* tonight?
嘿，今晚要不要各自付帳？

What a great idea! We'll split it 50-50.
好主意！五五分吧。

Sentence Patterns 句型練習

Do you want to share an appetizer?
你要一起分開胃菜嗎？

Let's go with the chicken wings.
我們選雞翅吧。

I've never eaten so much in my life.
我這輩子沒吃那麼多過。

Let's just split it 50-50.
五五分吧。

Vocabulary	字彙
☑ appetizer	開胃菜
☑ entrée	主菜
☑ dessert	點心
☑ splurge	揮霍
☑ house red	招牌紅酒
☑ tip	小費
☑ service charge	服務費
☑ go Dutch	各付各的

Clubs and Pubs
俱樂部與酒吧

MP3-45

Dialog 1

 主題 *Going out dancing.*
出去跳舞。

I've got a great idea. Let's go out dancing tonight!
我有個好主意。我們今晚出去跳舞！

You read my mind. It's been ages since I went dancing.

正合我意。我已經好久沒有去跳舞了。

I know a great club downtown. Their *grand opening* is tonight.

我知道鬧區有一間很棒的俱樂部。今晚有盛大的開幕慶祝。

Do they have a *cover charge*?
那兒會收入場費嗎？

Yes, it's NT$350. But it includes a drink.
會，收350元。但包含一份飲料。

That's not too bad then. Just give me a few minutes to get ready.

那還不賴。給我幾分鐘準備一下。

Dialog 2

主題 ▶ *Making a suggestion.*
給予建議。

 It's so *boring* to watch this baseball game at home.
在家看棒球賽超無聊的。

Why don't you go down to the sports pub?
你何不去那家運動酒吧？

They have a really nice *big screen TV.*
他們有超大豪華電視螢幕。

Yeah, I wouldn't mind a drink.
是唷，我想去喝一杯好了。

Do you mind if I join you?
你介意我跟你一起去嗎？

Of course not. But I had no idea you liked baseball.
當然不會介意。但我不知道你喜歡棒球。

I don't really. But their chicken wings are very tasty!
我沒有很喜歡。但那裡的雞翅膀很好吃。

Dialog 3

主題 ▶ *Ordering a drink at the bar.*
在吧台點飲料。

What can I get for you, young lady? A *pint of draught*?

小姐，你要些什麼？一杯飲料嗎？

Hmmm...I'm not sure. But definitely not beer.
嗯……我不太確定。但絕不要啤酒。

Well, people say I can make a really good *martini*.
呃，大家都說我調的馬丁尼很好喝。

Sounds good, but I don't like to taste the alcohol.
聽起來不錯，但我不想喝酒味太重的。

How about a strawberry *daiquiri* then? I'll make it extra fruity.

那草莓黛基利調酒如何？我會讓水果味重一點。

That sounds perfect. I'm sitting at the table near the front door.

好極了。我坐在靠前門的那張桌子。

Sentence Patterns 句型練習

🍎 You read my mind.
正合我意。

🍎 It's been ages since I went dancing.
我好久沒去跳舞了。

🍎 Do you mind if I join you?
你介意我跟你一起去嗎？

🍎 Sounds good, but I don't like to taste the alcohol.
聽起來不錯，但是我不想喝酒味太重的。

Vocabulary	字彙
☑ bouncer	彪形大漢
☑ cover charge	入場費
☑ grand opening	盛大開幕式
☑ boring	無聊的
☑ big screen TV	大螢幕電視
☑ pint of draught	一杯飲料
☑ martini	馬丁尼
☑ daiquiri	黛基利調酒

Shopping for CDs
買音樂CD

MP3-46

Dialog 1

  *Discussing **pirated** songs.*
討論盜版歌曲。

My CDs are all ***scratched***. I think it's time to stock up again.
我的CD都刮傷了。我想是該進貨的時候了。

Why don't you just download songs off the Internet? Everybody's doing it.
你為什麼不直接從網路上下載歌曲呢？大家都這樣做。

I just can't. I feel so ***guilty*** doing it. It's like stealing.
我就是不行。那讓我有罪惡感。好像偷東西一樣。

Not really. It's just like if I was sharing my CDs with you.
不完全吧。那就好像我分享我買的CD給你聽一樣。

Besides, it's totally free!
況且，這完全是免費的。

I know. But it's not about money.
我知道。但這跟錢完全沒有關係。

Besides, I love ***browsing*** through record stores.
而且，我很喜歡逛唱片行。

Me too. I can make a list of all the songs I want to download!

我也是。我可以在那裡列出一張所有我想要下載的歌曲清單。

Dialog 2

 主題 ▶ *Talking about music.*
談論音樂。

 What kind of music do you like?
你喜歡什麼樣的音樂？

 I'm a big jazz fan. But I've also got a good *selection* of *blues* CDs.

我是爵士樂的超級樂迷。但我也收集一套不錯的藍調音樂CD精選。

What about you?
那你呢？

 Me, I'm not too *fussy*. I like most pop songs on the radio.

我，我不太挑的。我喜歡大部分電台播放的流行歌曲。

 Who's your favorite artist?
你最喜歡的歌手是誰？

 Right now it's Avril Lavigne. But my favorite artist of all time is Madonna.

我現在喜歡艾薇兒。但我最喜歡的一直都是瑪丹娜。

Really? I grew up listening to her.
真的嗎？我聽她的歌長大的。

You're older than I thought.
你比我想的還要老。

But I'm still young at heart.
可是我的心仍年輕。

Dialog 3

主題　*Checking out a music CD.*
挑選音樂CD。

Are you going to buy that album?
你要買下那張專輯嗎？

I want to, but there are only two songs I like.
我想，可是我只喜歡其中兩首歌。

I know how you feel.
我可以體會你的感受。

It feels like you're *wasting* money buying a CD for just two songs.
就好像你浪費買整張CD的錢就為了那兩首歌。

Have you heard of how they're selling CDs in Germany?
你聽說過德國人是怎麼賣音樂CD的嗎？

Yeah, you can choose songs from *various* albums.
聽過，他們可以從不同專輯中挑一些歌曲。

Then they burn them all onto one CD.
然後燒成一張CD。

 Right. You end up paying the same price for one CD.

沒錯，那跟買一張音樂CD的價錢是一樣的。

But you buy only the songs you like.
但你只買了你喜歡的歌曲。

 I wonder why they don't do it here.
奇怪為何這裡不這樣做呢？

 Hmmm...sounds like a business idea?
嗯⋯⋯聽起來有商機可圖喔？

Sentence Patterns 句型練習

What kind of music do you like?
你喜歡什麼樣的音樂？

I'm a big jazz fan.
我是一個超級爵士樂迷。

You're older than I thought.
你比我想像中的還要老。

211

Have you heard of how they're selling CDs in Germany?

你聽說過德國人是怎麼賣音樂CD的嗎？

Vocabulary	字彙
☑ pirated	盜版的
☑ black market	黑市
☑ scratched	刮損的
☑ guilty	罪惡感
☑ browsing	瀏覽
☑ selection	精選集
☑ blues	藍調
☑ fussy	挑剔的
☑ wasting	浪費的
☑ various	不同的

Getting Around
到處逛逛

🔘 MP3-47

 Dialog 1

主題 ▶ *Buying a ticket for the MRT.*
買捷運車票。

 I've got a few hours before my flight.
離我的班機起飛還剩幾小時。

Can we check out Chiang Kai-Shek Memorial Hall?
我們可以去中正紀念堂看看嗎？

 Sure. The easiest way to get to there is on the MRT.
當然。去那最簡便的方法就是搭捷運。

There's a station across the street.
馬路對面有捷運站。

> They walk down into the MRT.
> 他們走進捷運站。

 How do I get a ticket?
我要怎樣購票。

 It's very simple. Just follow the *instructions* on the ticket *vending machine*.
很簡單。照售票機的步驟操作就可以了。

OK. First, I choose where I want to go...Then I *insert* my coins...

好，首先，先選擇想去的地點。然後投入錢幣⋯⋯

It's NT$30. But it'll give you change.

總共三十元。但是它會找你錢。

And there's my ticket. That was easy!

那就是我的票啦。真簡單。

Quick. The train is on its way.

快點，捷運來了。

Dialog 2

 主題

Asking for directions at the bus stop.
在公車站問路。

Excuse me. Which bus should I take to get to the zoo?

請問一下。去動物園要搭幾號公車？

I'm not sure. Let's take a look at this bus *schedule*.

我不確定。我們看一下公車時刻表吧。

I can't make heads or tails of it. What about you?

我分不清起站和終點站，你呢？

If this map is correct, the 530 and the 236 should get you there.

如果地圖沒錯的話，530和236號可以到達。

 Do I have to *transfer* anywhere?

我需要轉車嗎？

 I don't think so. They should take you right to the zoo.

不用吧。他們會直接載你到動物園。

 Dialog 3

主題

Giving directions to a taxi driver.
搭計程車報路。

In a taxi.
在計程車上。

 Where to, miss?

小姐，去哪？

 To Warner Village, please. I'm in a bit of a hurry too.

到華納影城，謝謝。我有點趕時間。

 You bet. Do you want me to take the freeway or Keelung Road?

沒問題。你想從快速道路去還是基隆路？

Don't you think Keelung Road will be busy right now?

你不覺得基隆路現在會很塞嗎？

Probably. If you're in a hurry we should take the freeway.

可能會。如果你趕時間我們可以開快速道路。

By the way, how much do you think the fare will be?

順便問一下，車資大約多少？

The *meter* starts at NT$70. By the time we get there, it should be about NT$250.

起跳是七十元，抵達時大概要兩百五十元。

OK. Just *step on it*! I'm really late.

好吧，快走吧。我已經遲到了。

Sentence Patterns 句型練習

Can we check out Chiang Kai-Shek Memorial Hall?

我們可以去中正紀念堂看看嗎？

Which bus should I take to get to the zoo?

去動物園要搭哪輛公車？

I can't make heads or tails of it.

我分不清起站和終點站。

By the way, how much do you think the fare will be?

順便問一下，車資大約多少？

Vocabulary	字彙
☑ **ferry**	渡船
☑ **instruction**	指示
☑ **vending machine**	售票機
☑ **insert**	插入
☑ **schedule**	時程表
☑ **transfer**	轉換
☑ **direction**	方向
☑ **meter**	儀表
☑ **step on it**	趕快

At a Bookstore
到書店

MP3-48

Dialog 1

主題▶ *Browsing through a bookstore.*
逛書局。

I just love this bookstore. I could spend days here.
我超喜歡這家書店。我可以成天待在這。

Me too. Hmmm...I can't decide whether to start in the *fiction* or non-fiction section.
我也是。嗯……我不知道要從小說區還是非小說區開始。

I'm heading straight for the *periodicals*.
我要直接去看期刊。

The new issue of National Geographic just came out.
最新一期「國家地理雜誌」剛發行。

I'll be in the *photography* section if you want to find me.
你可以在攝影區找到我。

That's right behind the periodicals, isn't it?
那是在期刊區後面，對吧。

No, it's in the art section. Beside films.
不是，是在藝術區。在電影區旁邊。

218

Dialog 2

 主題　*Discussing a book.*
討論書籍。

Don't you just love the smell of new books? Here, smell this!

你不覺得新書的味道很棒嗎？　來，聞聞看。

Obviously not as much as you. Are you going to buy that book or eat it?

很明顯地我沒有你那麼喜歡。你是要買書還是要吃書啊？

Don't be silly. I'm buying it. Just look at the *table of contents*.

別傻了。我要買。看看書的目錄吧。

Let's see...The World's Best Photos.
讓我看看……世界最棒的照片。

There's a chapter from each continent: Africa, North America...
有一章涵蓋各大洲：非洲、北美洲……

And there're also *tips* on how to improve my photography.

還有教我怎樣改進攝影技術的技巧呢！

Well, this sounds right up your alley.
這聽起來正合你的調調。

 Dialog 3

主題 *Summarizing a book.*
概述一本書。

I knew I'd find you in the World Literature section.
我就知道會在世界文學區找到你。

I'm debating whether or not to buy this one.
我正在為要不要買這本書傷腦筋。

It's called One Hundred Years of Solitude.
書名叫做「百年孤寂」。

That's a very famous book. I studied that in university.
那是一本很有名的書。我大學時讀過。

What's it about?
內容是什麼？

The summary says it's about a family in Latin America.
是在說一個拉丁美洲家族的故事。

That's where the *author* is from too.
那也正是作者的故鄉。

Hey, didn't he win the *Nobel Prize*?
嘿，那個作者不是得了諾貝爾文學獎嗎？

He sure did.
是啊。

This will probably be a good read then.
那這本書一定不錯。

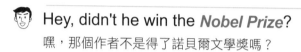

Sentence Patterns 句型練習

Don't you just love the smell of new books?
你不覺得新書的味道很棒嗎？

Don't be silly.
別傻了。

Well, this sounds right up your alley.
這聽起來正合你的調調。

I'm debating whether or not to buy this one.
我正在為要不要買這本書傷腦筋。

Vocabulary	字彙
☑ author	作者
☑ table of contents	書目
☑ fiction	小說
☑ periodical	期刊
☑ photography	攝影
☑ tip	技巧
☑ classic	古典的
☑ Nobel Prize	諾貝爾獎

MEMO

Listening to a Band

聽樂團演唱

🔊 MP3-49

Dialog 1

主題 ▶ *Talking about a new band.*
討論新樂團。

This band is really hot in Taiwan right now.
這個樂團現在在台灣正紅。

Yeah, I heard them on the radio. Their new *single debuted* in the Top 10.

沒錯，我在收音機上有聽到。他們的新單曲進入排行榜前十名。

Well, I just hope the radio doesn't play it to death. It's really a good song.

嗯，我只希望電台不要播到爛。它是首不錯的歌。

And I heard that their new album is not bad either.
我也聽說那張專輯不錯。

Well, let's check them out tonight. If they're any good, I'd like to buy it.

嗯，我們今晚去看看吧。如果真的不錯就買一張。

Who knows? They might just be another one-hit *wonder.*

誰知道呢？也有可能整張專輯只有一首好聽。

Dialog 2

 At a concert.
音樂會中。

These guys are really deafening! I can barely hear myself talk.

這些樂手真是吵死人了。我幾乎快聽不到自己說話的聲音了。

It serves you right for being in the first row.

你活該坐在第一排。

But I'm having a great time! The songs really keep you moving.

但是我正在享受啊。音樂很有動感。

Yeah, and the lead singer is so cool. He has real *presence*.

是的,主唱也很酷。他台風很好。

What did you think about the last song?

你覺得最後一首歌怎樣?

That was awesome. The drum solo was amazing.

真是棒極了。鼓的獨奏令人驚奇。

Well, I'm getting really sweaty. I'm going to get a drink.

嗯,我滿身是汗。我要去找些喝的。

You go ahead. I'll meet you at the bar.

你去吧。我待會去吧台找你。

Dialog ❸

 主題 *Hanging out at the bar.*
在吧台閒聊。

Is the band going to play another set?
樂團還要再表演一回嗎？

No, that's it. They're done for the night.
不，結束了。他們今晚不會再演奏了。

That's too bad. I was hoping to dance some more.
真可惜。我還想多跳一些舞。

Don't worry. Our *DJ* will be on in a few minutes.
別擔心。DJ 馬上就上場了。

What kind of music does he play?
他會放哪種音樂？

Mostly *hip-hop*.
大多是嘻哈音樂。

Great. I can stay out on the dance floor all night.
太棒了，我可以跳整晚了。

Then you'd better have a drink now. Here's a martini. It's *on the house*.
那你現在最好先喝一杯。來杯馬丁尼。本店招待。

Sentence Patterns　句型練習

Who knows?
誰知道？

It serves you right for being in the first row.
你活該坐在第一排。

I was hoping to dance some more.
我還想多跳一些舞。

Then you'd better have a drink now.
那你最好先喝一杯。

Vocabulary	字彙
☑ **fan**	歌（影）迷
☑ **single**	單曲
☑ **debut**	初次登台
☑ **one-hit wonder**	曇花一現
☑ **presence**	出場
☑ **hanging out**	閒逛
☑ **DJ**	唱片播放員
☑ **hip-hop**	嘻哈音樂
☑ **on the house**	免費（店家招待）

Going to a Surprise Birthday Party
驚喜生日派對

MP3-50

Dialog 1

主題 *Thinking of a birthday gift to buy someone.*
為壽星買生日禮物。

Are you going to Eric's birthday party?
你會去艾瑞克的生日派對嗎？

Yes, but I don't know what to get him.
會，但是我不知道要買什麼送他。

I'm *stumped* too. I know that he wants a new laptop computer, though.

我也想不出來。但是我知道他想要一台筆記型電腦。

Yeah, but I can't *afford* that. That's over NT$40,000!

嗯，但是我沒那麼多錢。一台要四萬多。

Hey, I've got a brilliant idea. Let's all *pitch in* and buy it for him!

嘿，我有個好主意。我們大家一起出錢買給他。

I'll get on the phone. I'm sure everyone will be excited about the idea.

我去打電話。相信大家都會覺得這個主意很好。

Dialog 2

主題 *Getting ready to surprise someone.*
準備給人驚喜。

You did such a wonderful job with this surprise party.

你將驚喜派對籌備得太棒了。

The decorations are beautiful.

佈置得很漂亮。

Thanks. I woke up very early to put up the balloons and *streamers*.

謝謝。我很早就起來佈置氣球和彩帶。

Do you need any help getting things ready?

你的準備工作需要任何幫忙嗎？

You could help me with the *punch*. It needs some fresh fruit.

你可以幫我弄水果酒。它需要放一些新鮮水果。

No problem. Uh-oh. There's no time. I hear *footsteps*.

沒問題。啊，來不及了。我聽到腳步聲了。

Quick! Everyone hides! He's coming!

快一點，大家躲起來。他來了！

Dialog 3

 主題 ▶ *Wishing some a happy birthday.*
祝你生日快樂。

Happy 30th Birthday, Eric!
艾瑞克，三十歲生日快樂！

Wow...30 years old already. I can't believe my *twenties* are over.

哇……已經三十歲了。真不敢相信我已經不再是二十幾歲的人了。

Here you go. This present is from me and Susan.
給你。這是我和蘇珊合送的禮物。

Oh, you shouldn't have.
喔，你們太多禮了。

What are you waiting for? Open it!
等什麼？快打開啊。

Hey! It's the Miles Davis Collection. Thank you so much.

嘿，是邁爾斯‧戴維斯的精選集。謝謝你們。

I just hope you like it.
希望你會喜歡。

Of course, I'll like it. You're so *thoughtful*.
當然，我很喜歡。你們真貼心。

Sentence Patterns 句型練習

I'll get on the phone.
我去打電話。

You did such a wonderful job with this surprise party.
你將驚喜派對籌備得太棒了。

I can't believe my twenties are over.
真不敢相信我已經不再是二十幾歲的人了。

Here you go.
這裡，拿去。

Vocabulary	字彙
☑ stumped	想不出來的
☑ afford	負擔
☑ pitch in	合力出資
☑ streamer	彩帶
☑ punch	水果酒
☑ footstep	腳步聲
☑ twenties	二十多歲
☑ thoughtful	貼心

Picnic in the Park

在公園內野餐

Dialog 1

 Looking for a place to picnic.
尋找野餐地點。

I just love being in *nature*. It's so peaceful.
親近大自然真好。感覺很寧靜。

And it's such a beautiful day today. There's not a cloud in the sky.
今天真是風和日麗。一點雲都沒有。

This is a nice *spot*. Let's set the picnic blanket down here.
這個地點很好。我們把野餐餐巾舖在這吧。

Can we move it under the tree instead? I'd rather be in the *shade*.
我們可以移到樹下嗎？我想待在樹蔭下。

Good idea. I burn easily.
好主意。我很容易曬傷。

Uh-oh. It looks like someone beat us here.
噢歐，這裡似乎有人不歡迎我們。

Someone and 10,000 of his friends.
某人和他的一萬位朋友。

How come ants always know when you're going to have a picnic?

為何螞蟻總是知道你什麼時候要野餐？

Dialog 2

 Cleaning up.
清理善後。

I'm stuffed! That was a great lunch!
我撐死了。午餐真棒。

Let's go for a stroll. I think I need to walk off all these calories.

我們去散步吧。這些卡路里需要消耗一下。

Let's clean up first. I don't want to leave any garbage behind.

先清理吧。我不想留下垃圾。

Yeah. Don't you hate people who *litter*?
是的。亂丟垃圾的人真討厭。

It's one of my *pet peeves*.
那是會令我生氣的事之一。

I don't think it's that difficult to throw your trash into the garbage can.

把垃圾丟到垃圾桶應該不會很困難。

Then let's *set a good example*. Here's a garbage bag.

那我們先做好榜樣吧。這裡有垃圾袋。

Dialog 3

主題 *Taking a photograph.*
拍照。

The *scenery* on this trail is amazing. The flowers are so colorful.

這條路上的風景真是美。有各種顏色的花。

This is a nice spot for a photo. Let's ask someone to take our photo.

這是個拍照的好地點。我們請人幫我們拍照。

That's ok. I've got a *tripod* in my bag. Just give me a minute.

不用了，我袋子裡有三角架。給我一分鐘。

It's a good thing you like to take photos.
你喜歡拍照真是件好事。

My camera is so old it doesn't even have an auto timer.
我的相機老舊得連自動計時的功能都沒有。

That's pretty old, alright. Ok, stand next to that rock.

果然很老舊。好了，站在石頭旁邊吧。

Over here?

這裡嗎？

Yes, ready? Here I come! Make room.

是的，準備好了嗎？我來了。移過去一點。

Say CHEEEEESE!

笑一個。

Sentence Patterns 句型練習

There's not a cloud in the sky.

天上一點雲都沒有。

Can we move it under the tree instead?

我們可以移到樹下嗎？

Just give me a minute.

給我一分鐘。

My camera is so old it doesn't even have an auto timer.

我的相機老舊得連自動計時的功能都沒有。

Vocabulary	字彙
☑ nature	大自然
☑ spot	景點
☑ shade	樹蔭
☑ litter	亂丟垃圾
☑ pet peeves	使人氣惱的事物
☑ set a good example	樹立好榜樣
☑ scenery	風景
☑ tripod	三角架

MEMO

MEMO

6

At Home
在家裡

The breaks during a TV program or movie are called commercial breaks. Many people don't bother to watch them. However, the companies behind the commercials still pay a lot of money for them. During the Super Bowl, companies paid US $2.2 million for a 30 second commercial!

電視節目和電影之間的休息時間叫做廣告時段。很多人懶得看廣告。然而，許多公司還是花大錢去作廣告。在超級盃舉行時，許多公司付兩百二十萬的錢作僅僅三十秒的廣告！！

Watching TV
看電視

 Dialog **1**

主題 *Fighting over the TV.*
搶電視。

James! **You're such a couch potato.** You've been *glued* to that TV all day long.

詹姆士，你真是個電視迷。你整天都黏在電視機前。

I can't help it. My favorite baseball team is playing today.

我忍不住嘛。我最喜歡的棒球隊今天比賽啊。

Well, you're gonna have to change the channel. Sex and the City is on.

不過，你得轉台了。慾望城市在播了。

No way. It's the bottom of the 8th inning. I can't miss the end of the game.

不要。已經第八局下半了，我不能錯過結局。

And I can't miss this *episode* either. Give me the *remote control*!

我也不能錯過這一集。遙控器給我！

Over my dead body!
除非我死！

Dialog 2

 主題 *Deciding what to watch.*
決定看什麼節目。

You really like to *channel surf*, don't you?
你很愛轉來轉去喔？

Well, there's nothing good on.
嗯，反正也找不到好看的。

There's an interesting show on the Discovery Channel.
探索頻道現在有個有趣的節目。

Actually, I'm just waiting for my favorite *soap opera* to start.
事實上我只是在等我最喜歡的連續劇開始。

I guess I'll just read a book now. But it's my turn after the soap opera.
我看我現在還是看我的書好了，但是連續劇完後換我看喔。

No problem. I'll let you know when it's over.
沒問題，演完了我再告訴你。

Dialog 3

 主題

Discussing your TV watching habits.
討論看電視習慣。

Do you think we should get *satellite* TV?
你覺得我們需要接衛星電視台嗎？

But we already get over 100 channels!
但是我們已經有一百多個頻道了。

Yes, but we don't watch most of them.
沒錯，但是幾乎都是我們不看的。

If we get a satellite, we'll have over a hundred good channels.
如果我們裝衛星電視就會有一百多台好節目。

If we get satellite TV, you won't do anything except watch TV.
如果我們裝衛星電視，你肯定什麼都不做只看電視。

You'll probably *skip* work to watch TV!
說不定你還蹺班回來看電視！

Hmmm...that does sound *tempting*, doesn't it?
嗯，聽起來真吸引人，不是嗎？

Well, I think it's a bad idea. We already watch too much TV.
算了，我不覺得那是個好主意。我們已經看太多電視了。

Sentence Patterns 句型練習

🍎 You're such a couch potato.
你真是個電視迷。

🍎 I can't help it.
我忍不住嘛。

🍎 Over my dead body!
除非我死！

🍎 But it's my turn after the soap opera.
連續劇過後換我看。

Vocabulary	字彙
☑ commercial	廣告
☑ glued	黏住的
☑ episode	（電視節目等）集
☑ remote control	遙控器
☑ channel surf	反覆轉電視台
☑ soap opera	連續劇
☑ satellite	衛星
☑ skip	跳過
☑ tempting	吸引人的

Using Computers
使用電腦

● MP3-53

 Dialog 1

主題▶ *Discussing the Internet.*
討論網際網路。

The Internet is so slow. Maybe we should get a faster *connection*.

網路連線好慢喔。也許我們該換速度快一點的連線。

I know. It's really frustrating. But our dial-up connection is cheap.

我知道。那真是令人沮喪。但是撥接比較便宜。

But we'll save so much time with *ADSL*.
可是用寬頻會省很多時間。

True. Then I wouldn't be afraid to load photos.
是啊。這樣我也可以放心下載圖片了。

Exactly. It wouldn't matter how long we spend *surfing* the net.

一點也沒錯。不管我們上網多久都沒關係。

It's settled then. We'll get ADSL next month.
那就這麼決定吧。我們下個月就改用寬頻。

Dialog 2

 Checking email.
收電子郵件。

Can I check my *email* on your computer?
我可以用你的電腦收信嗎？

Of course. Make yourself at home.
當然。請自便吧。

What do I do?
我該怎麼用？

Just close the window I'm working on. And then open Microsoft Explorer.
先關掉我在使用的視窗。然後開啟瀏覽器。

Thanks. Hey look! I've got ten unread *messages* in my *inbox*.
謝啦。嘿，快看。我的信箱裡有十封未讀信件。

I bet they're mostly junk mail like my account.
我打賭一定像我的一樣，大部分都是垃圾郵件。

Yes, but I've also got a message from my brother.
沒錯，但是我也收到我弟給我的信。

He sent me a photo. Take a look at this.
他寄給我一張照片。來看一下吧。

Oh, it's a photo of his baby. She's so cute.
喔，那是他小孩的照片。她好可愛喔。

Dialog 3

 主題 ▶ *Printing something off the computer.*
列印電腦檔案。

Do you mind if I print out this photo?
你介意我列印這張照片嗎？

Of course not. Maybe you should save it first.
當然不會。不過你應該先存檔。

Ok. Can you help me reduce the size first? I'm not very good with *graphics*.

你可以先幫我壓縮嗎？我對圖檔不太熟。

Sure. You just *click* on the photo and *drag* the corner like this...

沒問題。你先點一下那張圖，然後拖移，像這樣……

Now just print.
現在可以列印了。

Wow. It's almost like a real photo. Everything is so clear.

哇，看起來像真的照片一樣，很清楚耶。

Yes, today's printers are really amazing.
是的。現在的印表機列印效果都很棒。

Sentence Patterns 句型練習

It's settled then.
那就這麼決定吧！

Make yourself at home.
請自便吧。

I bet they're mostly junk mail like my account.
我打賭一定像我的一樣，大部分都是垃圾信件。

Maybe you should save it first.
你應該先存檔。

Vocabulary	字彙
☑ connection	連線
☑ ADSL	寬頻
☑ surfing	瀏覽
☑ email	電子信件
☑ messages	訊息
☑ inbox	電子訊息的總檔
☑ graphics	圖檔
☑ click	點選
☑ drag	拖引

◎ MP3-54

 Dialog 1

主題 ▶ *Discussing a new digital camera.*
討論新的數位相機。

Do you think it's time for a new digital camera?
你覺得現在適合買新的數位相機嗎？

What are you talking about? We just bought this last year!
你在說什麼？這台我們去年才剛買。

But I just saw an ad for the new model. It looks so much better.
可是我剛在廣告上看到最新型的。它看起來棒多了。

That's the problem with buying *electronics*. They become *obsolete* very quickly.
那就是買電子產品的缺點了，它們很快就過時了。

Then maybe we can get an *upgrade* instead. That would be cheaper.
那也許我們可以考慮升級，那樣會便宜些。

Or maybe you can just be happy with what you have. That would be easier.
或是你知足一點。這樣更簡單。

Dialog 2

 主題 *Discussing the CD player.*
討論CD播放器。

How many CDs can your CD player hold?
你的CD播放器一次可以裝多少片。

It holds up to 100 CDs.
大約一百片。

That's quite a few. I don't think I even own 50 CDs.
那不少耶。可是我總共還沒有五十張CD呢。

Actually, I don't either. I bought it for its sound quality. Have a listen.
事實上，我也沒有。我買它是因為音效很好。試聽一下吧。

Hey, that is pretty good. The sound is *crisp* and clear.
嘿，不錯耶。聲音很清晰。

Those are *high-end* speakers.
這是很高級的喇叭。

Dialog 3

主題 ▶ *Fixing the air conditioner.*
修冷氣。

What's making all that noise?
什麼聲音那麼吵？

The noise is coming from the air conditioning. I think it's time for a new one.

是冷氣發出的聲音。我看是該買新冷氣了。

Just let me have a look at it. All I need to do is put in a new *filter*.

先讓我瞧一瞧。只要換個新濾網就可以了。

Oh no you don't! Remember the last time you tried to fix something?

喔，千萬不要。記得上次你要修東西時發生的事嗎？

Are you saying I should call the repairman? Don't you trust me?

你是說我該請人來修嗎？你不信任我？

James, you try hard.
詹姆士，你是很努力在修。

But to be honest, you're *all thumbs* when you try to fix things.

但是老實說，你修東西時笨手笨腳的。

Sentence Patterns　句型練習

Do you think it's time for a new digital camera?

你覺得現在適合買新的數位相機嗎？

What are you talking about?

你在說什麼？

Have a listen.

試聽一下吧。

Remember the last time you tried to fix something?

記得上次你要修東西時發生的事嗎？

Vocabulary	字彙
☐ **electronics**	電器
☐ **obsolete**	過時的；老舊的
☐ **upgrade**	升級
☐ **crisp**	清脆的
☐ **high-end**	高檔貨
☐ **filter**	濾網
☐ **all thumbs**	笨手笨腳的

Housework
家事

MP3-55

Dialog 1

主題 *Doing the dishes.*
洗碗盤。

Whose turn is it to do the dishes?
今天換誰洗碗盤？

I did them last night. So, it's your turn now.
我昨晚洗過了。所以今天換你。

Really? I could swear that I just did them.
真的嗎？我可以發誓我剛洗過。

If you hate doing dishes so much, why don't you buy a dishwasher?
如果你這麼討厭洗碗，何不買部洗碗機？

I don't hate it. I just think you do a much better job than me.
我不討厭洗碗。我只是覺得你洗得比我好。

You don't mean that! You just don't want to do the dishes!
你才不是說真的。你只是不想洗碗。

Dialog 2

 主題 *Recycling garbage.*
垃圾回收。

The city's new *recycling* schedule sure is *confusing*. What can be recycled?

城裡的回收時間排的很混亂。哪些是可以回收的？

Almost everything. We have to *separate plastics*, glass bottles, and *cardboard*.

幾乎所有東西都可以。我們必須把塑膠、玻璃瓶和紙板分類。

What about batteries? Do we throw that in the trash?

那電池呢？我們要丟到垃圾堆裡嗎？

I believe they *recycle* batteries, but I'm not sure which days.

我相信電池也有回收，但是我不確定是哪天。

I wonder if other people are just as confused.

我猜想其他人一定也搞不清楚。

Well, it shouldn't be so difficult. We should just ask someone.

嗯，應該不會太難。我們應該找人問問。

Dialog 3

 主題 *Doing the laundry.*
洗衣服。

Do you want me to put your silk blouse in with the rest of the *laundry*?

你要我把你的絲質上衣和其它衣服一起洗嗎？

Of course not! It's very *delicate*.

當然不行！它質料很細緻。

Then I'll leave it *aside* for you to hand wash.

那我把它分開讓你手洗。

OK. I'll do it later. Please remember to separate the colors and the whites.

好吧，我等一下去洗。請記得，有顏色的衣服和白色的衣服要分開洗。

I've already done so. I'm bleaching the whites as we speak.

我已經分類了，我們在說話時我已經在漂白了。

Thanks for doing the *laundry*, James.

詹姆士，謝謝你幫我洗衣服。

Sentence Patterns 句型練習

Whose turn is it to do the dishes?
今天換誰洗碗盤？

I could swear that I just did them.
我可以發誓我剛洗過。

If you hate doing dishes so much, why don't you buy a dishwasher?
如果你這麼討厭洗碗盤，怎麼不買一部洗碗機？

I'm bleaching the whites as we speak.
我們在說話時，我已經在漂白了。

Vocabulary	字彙
☑ housework	家事
☑ laundry	待洗衣物
☑ recycling	回收
☑ confusing	混淆的
☑ separate	分開
☑ plastics	塑膠
☑ cardboard	紙板
☑ delicate	細緻
☑ aside	放一邊

Pets
寵物

MP3-56

Dialog 1

 Telling someone about a pet.
討論寵物。

Shelley, meet my *hamster* Shakespeare.
雪利，來見見我養的黃金鼠莎士比亞。

He's so cute. What does he eat?
好可愛喔。他吃什麼？

Oh, Shakespeare eats everything. He especially likes dried fruit.
喔，莎士比亞什麼都吃。他特別喜歡吃乾水果。

Actually, he doesn't seem to be eating his food.
事實上，牠好像沒在吃牠的食物。

No. He likes to *store* everything in his *cheeks*. That's why he looks so fat.
沒錯，牠喜歡把食物存在頰囊裡，所以看起來才會那麼胖。

Look at the poor thing. He runs around in his wheel but doesn't go anywhere.
看看那可憐的小東西，牠一直在滾輪上跑，可是哪也去不了。

Do you want to take him out of the *cage*?
你想把牠放出籠子嗎？

Sure! Can I?
當然！可以嗎？

Dialog 2

 Discussing pet fish.
討論寵物魚。

What a lovely fish *tank* you have.
好可愛的魚缸喔。

Thanks. I really love my fish. I talk to them every day.

謝謝。我真的很愛我的魚，我每天都跟牠們說話。

How many do you have?
你有幾隻？

I've got four *goldfish* and 3 angel fish.
我有四隻金魚和三隻天使魚。

I used to have four of each but one just died.
我以前各有四隻，不過一隻最近剛死。

That's too bad.  I see you've also got a turtle, too.
真遺憾。我看到你還有一隻烏龜。

Yes, who do you think killed the fish?
是的，你認為是誰害死那隻魚？

Dialog 3

 主題 ► *Taking the dog out for a walk.*
溜狗。

Bobo is *barking*. I think it's time for her to go for a walk. Do you mind?

波波在叫了。我想溜狗時間到了。你介意帶牠去嗎？

Of course not. I could use some exercise too.

當然不會。我可以順便出去運動。

Please make sure she goes to the bathroom before coming back.

請在帶牠回來前確定牠有大小便。

I know. Otherwise she'll wake us up in the *middle of the night*.

我知道。不然的話牠會在半夜把我們吵醒。

Sentence Patterns 句型練習

He especially likes dried fruit.
他特別喜歡吃乾水果。

I see you've also got a turtle, too.
我看到你還有一隻烏龜。

I could use some exercise too.
我可以順便出去運動。

🍎 Please make sure she goes to the bathroom before coming back.

請在帶牠回來前確定牠有大小便。

Vocabulary	字彙
☑ hamster	黃金鼠
☑ store	儲存
☑ cheek	臉頰
☑ cage	籠子
☑ tank	魚缸
☑ goldfish	金魚
☑ barking	狗吠聲
☑ middle of the night	半夜

MEMO

....

....

....

....

At the supermarket
在超市

MP3-57

主題 *Making a shopping list.*
擬定購物清單。

The fridge is totally empty. We need to make a trip to the supermarket.

冰箱完全空空的。我們必須去超市一趟。

Let's make a shopping list first. I don't want to buy things we don't need.

讓我們先擬定購物單吧。我不想買不需要的東西。

OK. We need eggs, *instant noodles*, and some orange juice.

好吧。我們需要雞蛋、泡麵，和一些柳橙汁。

We also need to buy some snacks. I can't watch TV without snacks.

我們也需要買一些點心。我看電視不能不吃零食。

I'm going on a *diet*. I don't want any *junk food*.

我要減肥。我不想吃垃圾食物。

Well, that just means there's more for me!

好吧，那我只好多吃點嘍。

Dialog 2

 主題 *Shopping for fruits and vegetables.*
購買水果和蔬菜。

Let's start with fruits and vegetables. What do we need?

先從蔬菜和水果開始買。我們需要什麼？

Let's have salad tonight. Remember, I'm going on a diet.

今晚吃生菜沙拉吧。請記得我要減肥。

So, we need lettuce, carrots, tomatoes, *cucumbers*...what else?

所以我們需要萵苣、紅蘿蔔、蕃茄、小黃瓜……還有什麼？

I really like *alfalfa sprouts* in my salad. Can we get some?

我想要在沙拉裡加苜蓿芽。可以買一些嗎？

I'm not a big fan, but go ahead.
我不是很喜歡，但是你去拿吧。

Now for the fruit. Let's get some mangoes and *papaya*.

現在來買水果。我們買些芒果和木瓜吧。

Would you be angry if I bought some durian?

如果我買榴槤，你會生氣嗎？

 No, but don't expect me to eat it with you.

不會，但是別期望我和你一起吃。

 Dialog 3

 主題 *Buying meat.*

買肉類。

 Hmmm...our shopping *cart* is already getting quite full.

嗯……我們的購物車已經很滿了。

Is there anything else we need?

還有什麼要買的嗎？

 We haven't bought any meat yet. Let's get some *fresh* fish and some chicken.

我們還沒買肉。我們買些新鮮的魚和一些雞肉吧。

 I'd rather get *frozen* fish. They're much easier to cook.

我寧願買冷凍魚。它們好煮多了。

 True. And since we're in the frozen foods section, maybe we can pick up some ice cream.

沒錯。既然我們在冷凍食品區，也可以買些冰淇淋。

Wait a minute. Didn't you just say you were on a diet?

等一下。你不是說你在減肥嗎？

I said I'm going on a diet. I didn't say that I was on a diet.

我說我要減肥。我沒說我在減肥。

So, I'll just start it next week.

所以我下星期再開始。

Sentence Patterns 句型練習

We need eggs, instant noodles, and some orange juice.

我們需要雞蛋、泡麵、和一些柳橙汁。

I'm not a big fan, but go ahead.

我不是很喜歡，但是你請便。

Would you be angry if I bought some durian?

如果我買榴槤，你會生氣嗎？

I'd rather get frozen fish.

我寧願買冷凍魚。

Vocabulary	字彙
☑ bakery	麵包
☑ instant noodles	泡麵
☑ diet	節食
☑ junk food	垃圾食物
☑ cucumber	小黃瓜
☑ alfalfa sprout	苜蓿芽
☑ papaya	木瓜
☑ cart	推車
☑ fresh	新鮮的
☑ frozen	冷凍的

M E M O

UNIT 7 Cooking

烹飪

Dialog 1

主題 *Checking the ingredients.*
食材確認。

Let's stay home tonight. We haven't had a home-cooked meal in weeks.

我們今晚待在家裡吧。我們好幾個禮拜都沒有在家吃了。

You're right. I can cook up a nice chicken *curry*.

對呀，我可以做道美味的咖哩雞。

Uh...I don't think my stomach can handle anything spicy today.

呃……我想今天我不能吃辣的食物。

Then how about pasta? Do we have all the ingredients for *spaghetti*?

那義大利麵如何？我們有義大利麵的食材嗎？

OK! Let's make sure we've got what we need.

好吧！我們先確定所有食材都齊了。

We need tomato sauce, onions, *ground beef*, mushrooms...

我們需要蕃茄醬、洋蔥、碎牛肉、蘑菇……

Stop! All this talk is making me hungry. Let's just cook!

好了！這樣長篇大論只會讓我更餓。我們直接開始煮吧！

Dialog **2**

主題

Making spaghetti sauce.
製作義大利麵醬料。

OK. We've got all the *ingredients*. What's first?

好了，食材都齊了。先要怎麼作呢？

Let me check the recipe. It says we need to *dice* the onions and tomatoes.

我來看看食譜吧。上面寫説我們要先將洋蔥及蕃茄切丁。

Done. Now it says "Put some *oil* in a sauce pan. Sauté onions and *ground beef*."

做好了。現在是「在醬料平底鍋內放些油，將洋蔥及碎牛肉下鍋翻炒。」

What in the world is Sauté?

「翻炒」到底是什麼意思？

I'm not really sure. I think it's just a fancy word for *fry*. Don't worry about it.

我不太確定耶。我想應該是炒菜的雅字吧！別管它。

Well, the ground beef looks like it's done. What now?

好啦，碎牛肉似乎炒好了。接下來呢？

Now you just *pour* in the tomato sauce and you're done.

現在你把蕃茄醬倒進去就完成了。

Dialog 3

 主題

Cooking the noodles.
烹煮麵條。

You work on the *spaghetti* sauce. I'll *boil* the noodles.
你來做義大利麵醬料，我來煮麵條。

Don't forget to add a *pinch* of salt to the water. It helps it to boil.

別忘了在水裡加一把鹽巴。水可以比較快煮沸。

I sure will. Are you hungry tonight? Should I cook you a lot?

我一定會的。你今晚很餓嗎？我是不是應該煮多一些？

Cook me a lot. And whatever we don't finish we can eat as *leftovers* tomorrow.

煮多一些吧。反正今天沒吃完的明天可以將當剩菜吃。

They continue cooking.
他們繼續烹飪中。

The noodles are ready. Can I have a taste of the sauce? Mmmm...it's delicious.

麵條好了。我可以嚐一嚐醬料嗎？嗯，很美味。

Then let's set the table. It's time to eat.
那我們來擺餐具吧。該開動了。

Sentence Patterns 句型練習

🍎 I don't think my stomach can handle anything spicy today.
我想我今天不能吃辣的食物。

🍎 Let's make sure we've got what we need.
我們先確定所有東西都齊了。

🍎 What in the world is sauté?
「翻炒」到底是什麼意思？

🍎 Don't forget to add a pinch of salt to the water.
別忘了在水中加一把鹽巴。

Vocabulary	字彙
☑ ingredients	食材
☑ curry	咖哩
☑ spaghetti	義大利麵
☑ dice	丁狀物
☑ oil	油
☑ ground beef	碎牛肉
☑ fry	炒
☑ pour	倒
☑ boil	煮沸
☑ pinch	一撮
☑ leftover	剩菜

Running Errands

處理雜務

Dialog 1

主題 *Paying bills.*
繳帳單。

 Well, it's that time of the month again.
喔，又是每個月的這時候了。

 Don't remind me. The bills just keep adding up.
別提醒我啦。帳單就是越來越多。

 There are two bills *due* today: the water and the *electricity*.

今天有兩筆帳單要付：水費和電費。

I'll go to the bank this afternoon.

我今天下午就會去銀行處理。

 Thanks. The telephone and Internet bills aren't *due* until next week.

謝謝。電話和網路帳單要到下週才到期。

 And let's not forget to call the *landlord. Rent* is *due* tomorrow.

別忘了要打電話給房東。房租明天就該付了。

 Oh, don't worry. If we forget he'll come looking for us.

喔，別擔心。我們要是忘了他會來找我們的。

Dialog 2

 主題 *Going to the bank.*
到銀行去。

Excuse me. Both your bank machines are *out of order*.

抱歉。你們兩台提款機都故障了。

They're being fixed at the moment. Is there anything I can help you with?

等一下就修好了。我可以幫你什麼嗎？

I just want to *withdraw* some money. Do I need to fill out a form?

我只想要提錢。我要填什麼單子嗎？

Yes. Please write your *account* number here. And sign here at the bottom.

是的。請將你的帳號寫在這裡，然後在底下這裡簽名。

Here you go. Could I have that in 500s and 1000s please?

拿去吧。請換五百和一千元鈔票給我好嗎？

Certainly. That's 1000, 2000, 2500...
好的。這裡是一千、兩千、兩千五百……

Dialog 3

主題

Going to the post office.
到郵局去。

Hello. I'd like to mail this *parcel* to England.
哈囉。我想郵寄這包裹到英國。

Would you like that *express* or regular?
你要寄快遞還是平信？

That depends on how long they take.
那就要看郵寄要花多久時間。

Regular service takes 3 to 6 weeks. Express takes about 5 days.

平信的話要三到六週。快遞則五天就到了。

Then I'll definitely send it express. How much is it with *insurance*?

那我當然要寄快遞。再加上保險的話要多少錢呢？

With insurance, it comes out to NT$500. Please fill out this form.

加上保險，總共要五百元。請填一下這張表。

Sentence Patterns　句型練習

🍎 Don't remind me.
別提醒我。

🍎 Is there anything I can help you with?
我可以幫你什麼嗎？

🍎 That depends on how long they take.
那就要看花多久時間。

🍎 Then I'll definitely send it express.
那我當然要寄快遞。

Vocabulary	字彙
☑ rent	租金
☑ landlord	屋主；地主
☑ deposit	押金
☑ due	到期的
☑ electricity	電
☑ out of order	失效；故障
☑ withdraw	提款
☑ account	帳戶
☑ parcel	包裹
☑ express	快遞
☑ insurance	保險

 MP3-60

 Discussing ways to lose weight.
討論減重的方法。

 I think I'm getting a bit of a *belly*. What do you think?

我想我有點小肚子了。你覺得呢？

 Hmmm...you have been getting a little bit fat lately.
嗯……你最近是有些胖了。

Why don't you exercise a bit more?
你為何不多做一些運動？

 I'm just not very *motivated*.
我就是提不起勁來。

But I saw an exercise machine on TV. I might order that.
但我在電視上看到一台運動機，我可能會訂購一台。

 You mean the one that helps you lose *weight* while you watch TV?
你是說那個可以讓你邊看電視邊減重的機器嗎？

 Yeah, do you think it will work?
是的，你覺得那有效嗎？

The only thing that it will do is *rip you off*.

那只會浪費你的錢而已。

If you really want to lose weight, let's go jogging tomorrow.

你若是真的想要減重的話，我們明天就去慢跑吧。

Dialog 2

主題

Going jogging.

慢跑去。

Ok. I'm ready to go. How many miles are we doing this morning?

好了，我準備好了。我們今天早上要跑多少哩？

Hold your horses! First, we need to *stretch*.

稍安勿躁。我們得先伸展一下。

Isn't stretching for people who are *out of shape*?

伸展操不是給身體狀況差的人做的嗎？

Of course not! It warms up your muscles. It also keeps you from getting *injured*.

當然不是。它可以讓你暖身及舒緩肌肉，還可以讓你避免受傷。

Ouch! I never knew stretching could hurt so much.

喔，我從來不知道伸展操會這麼痛啊！

You know what they say: "No pain no gain".
你這才知道所謂的「一分耕耘，一分收穫」啊！

Dialog 3

主題 *Asking for a break.*
要求休息一下。

Wendy...I...I can't *keep up.* Let's take a break.
溫蒂……我……我跟不上了。我們休息一下吧。

But James. We've *barely* made it around the block. You can't be tired yet.
但是詹姆士，我們還沒繞街道一圈呢。你不可能會累的。

Just two minutes. I want to *catch my breath*.
兩分鐘就好了。我需要喘一下。

Ok. But not too long though. Your muscles will get cold again.
好吧，但是別太久。你的肌肉會再度冷下來的。

OK. I can feel my legs again. Let's go.
好，我的腳又恢復知覺了。我們走吧。

That's the spirit! I'll race you to the corner!
就是這個精神！我們一起賽跑到轉角吧！

Sentence Patterns 句型練習

If you really want to lose weight, let's go jogging tomorrow.
你若真的想要減重,我們明天就去慢跑。

Hold your horses!
稍安勿躁!

I never knew stretching could hurt so much.
我從來不知道做伸展操會這麼痛。

That's the spirit!
就是這個精神!

Vocabulary	字彙
☑ belly	肚子
☑ motivated	被激發的
☑ weight	重量
☑ rip you off	花你一大筆錢的
☑ stretch	伸展
☑ out of shape	身體狀況不佳
☑ injured	受傷的
☑ keep up	跟上
☑ barely	幾乎不
☑ catch my breath	喘口氣

Decorating the House
佈置房子

 MP3-61

Dialog 1

主題 *Putting together a new shelf.*
組裝新架子。

I've bought a new bookshelf from Ikea. Can you help me put it together?
我從「宜家」買了一個新書架。你可以幫我組起來嗎？

Sure. What kind of tools do you need?
好啊。你需要什麼工具呢？

The instructions are impossible to read.
我完全看不懂說明書耶。

It can't be that difficult.
那沒那麼困難。

We'll just need a *screwdriver* to screw the *boards* together.
我們只需要一個螺絲起子將板子用螺絲鎖起來。

Wow. That was easy. Now we just need to *hammer* in these few nails and we're done.
哇，那很容易。現在我們只要將這幾個釘子槌進去就完成了。

Hey, that's a pretty good looking shelf. It will look great in the living room.
嘿，這架子還蠻漂亮的。放在客廳裡會很好看。

Dialog 2

 主題 *Trying to help a sick plant.*
嘗試著去救將枯死的植物。

Since we're redecorating the living room, why don't we get a new plant?

既然我們在重新佈置客廳，我們何不買株新植物呢？

Yeah. Look at that poor thing. All the leaves are dry.

是啊，看看那可憐的東西。它所有的葉子都乾掉了。

It's probably not getting enough water.

大概是沒有澆足夠的水。

Sure it is. I make sure to water it every morning.

當然足夠。我可是每天早上都有澆水。

Then maybe we need to move it out onto the *balcony*.

或許我們得將它移到陽台去。

Lack of sunlight might be the problem.

問題可能是出在缺乏陽光。

No, I just think it needs to be replanted. I'll get some *soil* from the supermarket.

不，我想它可能只需要重新栽種，我去超市買些土回來。

Dialog 3

 主題 *Decorating the living room.*
佈置客廳。

Our living room looks much better now.
我們的客廳現在看起來好多了。

I really like the new plant and new shelf.
我真的很喜歡新的植物和新的架子。

But there's still something missing. I think we should *spice up* the walls a little.
但還缺乏一些東西。我想我們應該讓牆壁添些趣味。

What do you mean? I just put up that L.A. Lakers *poster*.
什麼意思？我才剛把洛杉磯湖人隊的海報貼上去。

That's not my idea of beauty. I was thinking of getting an Ansel Adams picture.
我的美麗不是指那個。我想要放張安賽・亞當斯的攝影作品。

Oh, I've heard of him. Isn't he that black and white photographer?
喔，我聽過他。他不是那個黑白攝影師嗎？

Yes. He's one of my favorites.
是的。他是我最喜歡的攝影師之一。

Ok. As long as I don't have to take down my Kobe Bryant poster.

好吧！只要不拿下我的柯比・布萊恩的海報就沒問題。

Oh my. I don't know how I *put up with* you.

喔，天啊！我真不知道我是如何忍受你的。

Sentence Patterns 句型練習

The instructions are impossible to read.
我完全看不懂說明書。

I make sure to water it every morning.
我確定我每天早上都有替它澆水。

Lack of sunlight might be the problem.
問題可能是出在缺乏陽光。

That's not my idea of beauty.
我對美麗的概念不是這樣的。

Vocabulary	字彙
☑ pre-assembled	事先組好的
☑ screwdriver	螺絲起子
☑ board	板子
☑ hammer	榔頭
☑ balcony	陽台
☑ soil	土壤
☑ spice up	增添風趣
☑ poster	海報
☑ put up (with)	忍受

MEMO

國家圖書館出版品預行編目資料

可以馬上學會的超強英語句型課/蘇盈盈,
珊朵拉合著. -- 新北市：哈福企業有限公
司, 2020.12
　面；　公分. -- (英語系列；68)
ISBN 978-986-99161-7-2(平裝附光碟片)
1.英語 2.句法
805.169　　　　　　　　　109019124

英語系列：68

書名 / 可以馬上學會的超強英語句型課
合著 / 蘇盈盈・卡拉卡
出版單位 / 哈福企業有限公司
責任編輯 / Mary Chang
封面設計 / Lin Lin House
內文排版 / Co Co
出版者 / 哈福企業有限公司
地址 / 新北市板橋區五權街 16 號
封面內文圖 / 取材自 Shutterstock

email ／ welike8686@Gmail.com
電話／（02）2808-4587
傳真／（02）2808-6245
出版日期／ 2020 年 12 月
台幣定價／ 330 元
港幣定價／ 110 元
Copyright © Harward Enterprise Co., Ltd

總代理／采舍國際有限公司
地址／新北市中和區中山路二段 366 巷 10 號 3 樓
電話／（02）8245-8786
傳真／（02）8245-8718

Original Copyright © EDS Culture Co., Ltd.

哈福

哈福